TEXAS FRIDAYS

DALLAS

SAM MOUSSAVI

EPIC
Press

Dallas
Texas Fridays

Written by Sam Moussavi

Copyright © 2017 by Abdo Consulting Group, Inc.

Published by EPIC Press™
PO Box 398166
Minneapolis, MN 55439

Cover design by Kali Yeado
Images for cover art obtained from iStockPhoto.com
Edited by Gil Conrad

LIBRARY OF CONGRESS CATALOGING-IN-PUBLICATION DATA

Names: Moussavi, Sam, author.
Title: Dallas / by Sam Moussavi.
Description: Minneapolis, MN : EPIC Press, 2017. | Series: Texas Fridays
Summary: Bobby Dupree, a senior at Trinity High, has always been a backup quarterback
    and never expected to see the field during his final season. But when his team's starting
    quarterback goes down, things change for Bobby as he is thrust into the starting role.
Identifiers: LCCN 2016946208 | ISBN 9781680764925 (lib. bdg.) |
    ISBN 9781680765489 (ebook)
Subjects: LCSH: High school—Fiction. | Football—Fiction. | Football players—Fiction. | Life
    change events—Fiction. | Young adult fiction.
Classification: DDC [Fic]—dc23
LC record available at http://lccn.loc.gov/2016946208

EPIC
Press

EPICPRESS.COM

For those eager to take liberties with the imagination and stay awhile.

—Pete Simonelli

1

BOBBY DUPREE WAS A BACKUP QUARTERBACK. IT didn't bother him that this was his position on the Trinity High School varsity football team. Even off the football field, Bobby was a backup quarterback kind of guy. Not everyone was meant to be a star. It was neither desire nor politics that held Bobby back—he surely wanted to see the field. What football player doesn't? And in truth, he'd always had every opportunity to earn the right to start. Bobby was smart enough to recognize his place in Trinity's quarterback pecking order: second string. The station in life he had earned.

"You ready to ride the bench again this year, Dupree?" Edmond asked.

Edmond Daniels was the starting quarterback at Trinity. He was a junior, like Bobby, but had long bypassed Bobby on the depth chart. Edmond was fast, and possessed a cannon for an arm.

"Yeah, whatever," Bobby said, trying not to react to Edmond's grin, which accompanied every one of his well-timed digs.

It was the first practice of the season, and Trinity was expecting big things. The high school football scene in Dallas was highly competitive, just like in the rest of the state. Trinity held the preseason optimism that was commonplace for most teams in Dallas. Edmond Daniels was Trinity's most potent weapon. He would create separation from the rest of the Dallas pack and give Trinity a real chance in the playoffs. Edmond only got better with each snap he took, finishing his sophomore year with a stat line of twenty total touchdowns—eleven running and nine throwing—and only three interceptions. And that was just in spot-starting duty. It was clear now that the team would go as far as Edmond could take it.

"You know TCU is lookin' at me, right, Dupree?" Edmond asked.

"I didn't know that," Bobby said.

"But I'm lookin' for something better," he said. "I wanna get up out of Texas."

Bobby just nodded. He didn't have to dream of getting out of Texas. Bobby had been out of the state many times in his life. He'd even been out of the country more times than he could remember.

"Just gotta stay healthy," Edmond said, before bowing his head and whispering a little prayer. Not the Lord's prayer, just a little something that Edmond cooked up himself to feel safe.

Edmond grabbed his helmet and ran out onto the field. Bobby grabbed his helmet and followed suit. Bobby didn't have a problem being in Edmond's shadow. He wanted to play, of course, but felt that Edmond deserved this moment.

The field behind the school was immaculate—a

testament to the school's groundskeeper who was kept on staff year round. The turf had that awe-inspiring look and feel of a football field before it is taken over by twenty-two players and torn to shreds. The team was on the field under the ubiquitous August sun. Defensive backs were talking smack to receivers and vice versa. Offensive linemen were mostly quiet in their pudgy stoicism. Bobby stood next to Edmond and the third quarterback, Mickey Montoya, a freshman from Arlington. The trio stretched out their calves, quads, and hip flexors. Edmond lorded over the rest of the team because he could. Bobby simply worried about loosening up.

About five minutes later, the coaching staff graced the perfectly green field of battle. The head coach, Brett "Stud" Davis, was the last one out. He was a rock star in the Dallas high school football scene and one of the youngest head coaches to be named head football coach in Dallas, and the youngest one to ever win a Texas Six-A Division

One championship. But the second championship had so far proven to be elusive.

Brett—or "Stud" as he preferred—was now looking over his shoulder.

"Let's get to it!" Stud called out.

The whole team met in a circle around the fifty-yard line. Stud was in the middle of the circle, looking outward, scanning the entire three hundred and sixty degrees. He spat, blew his whistle, and then pointed in the direction of the team helpers standing in the eastern end zone. Country music filled the space in and around the field, and the whole team laughed. If there was anything that Stud pined for more than winning another Texas Six-A Division One championship, country music would be that thing.

"Oklahoma drill!" Stud yelled over the sounds of shrill guitars and beer-soaked lyrics.

The circle tightened around Stud and suddenly there was less air to breath, and even less time to make sense of it all.

"Degarmo!" Stud howled. "You and Mundy first!"

The circle growled and constricted further. Troy Degarmo was Trinity's mammoth left tackle, already committed to the University of Arkansas. Alton Mundy was a talented, but not always productive, defensive tackle. They squared off in the center of the circle, and besides Kenny Chesney and the circle's chants for blood, not another sound could be heard.

Underneath the shoulder pads of both Degarmo and Mundy, there was the ever-present thumping of their hearts. Every football player felt this sensation before stepping on the field; the inherent danger of the sport would never allow for relaxation, no matter how seasoned the players. This feeling was only amplified when put on display in the Oklahoma Drill.

Degarmo took his three-point stance, and Mundy took a four-point stance. Stud let them get set. The anticipation rattled both in and out of the circle. Degarmo flexed his left hand. Sweat poured down Mundy's face as he looked down at the grass and counted a few individual blades.

Stud blew his whistle and then there was thunder. The two players went for it because this was no place to show weakness. The drill was meant to instill competition, yet there was a more primal motive on display as well. A player could not back down from another player lest he be weeded out. The tone for the season depended on this process. The more players who were weeded out early, the better off the team would be.

After the initial stalemate, Degarmo overpowered Mundy and drove him back into the circle. Mundy was lifted off his feet and planted on his back. Stud blew his whistle and ran over to Degarmo, smacking him on the helmet and whipping the circle into a frenzy.

Mundy was forgotten. Beaten. Fallen. The only person who cared for him was Bobby Dupree. Bobby broke away and helped Mundy to his feet. The defensive tackle's shoulders slumped, and

Bobby got up on his tippy-toes to give him a pat on the back of the helmet.

Stud turned around and assessed Mundy solemnly, as if his player had died a little in his eyes. "What do you say, Mundy?" Stud asked. He was charged up, eyes bouncing around skittishly.

"I need a minute, Coach."

"You need a what?" Stud asked, moving in. "He just whipped you, son."

Mundy looked around at the circle and saw the eyes inside it advancing on him, gaining information on him, with the intention of weeding him out. He nodded and took his place again in front of Degarmo.

And the Oklahoma Drill went on.

2

"**P**UT A LITTLE AIR UP UNDER THAT THROW, ED," Stud called out to Edmond, before ignoring Bobby's perfectly arched go-route during his rep.

Edmond got most of the reps during practice because he was the starter and needed the reps to get into the flow of the offense. It's not that Bobby didn't throw a pretty ball. He did. The problem was, Bobby's pretty throws always occurred in practice, and usually with the defense going half-speed. Bobby tapped Edmond on the shoulder before Mickey Montoya took a rare third quarterback rep.

"I thought the throw was good, Ed," Bobby said.

"When the corner's off, it's good to throw it on a rope like that."

"Well, Stud's always gotta say somethin'," Edmond said, flashing his million-dollar smile.

Edmond took the next seven reps before Bobby took another one. It was easy to see why Edmond was the starter and why Bobby was not. Edmond looked like a football player. His body was packed and ripped from hours upon hours spent in the weight room. His speed was otherworldly, like God himself had kissed his calves and given them His blessing for gridiron greatness. One other attribute really set Edmond apart, and not just from Bobby. He *could* throw the ball. Edmond wasn't a one-trick quarterback, who always looked to run. As a black quarterback, Ed went out of his way to make sure that this stereotype did not apply to him. Edmond could stand in the pocket. He could read a defense. And when he set his feet, he could spin it with the best quarterbacks Texas had to offer, white or black.

Bobby, on the other hand, looked like a backup.

There was no definition to speak of on his frame. His foot speed was average, on a good day, and his arm strength was so-so. The only thing Bobby had going for him was that he had experience being a backup. When a player has experience being a backup, he usually finds himself on the second or third unit, watching a lot of football. Though he never dared to say it out loud, Bobby hoped that somehow, some way, all that watching he had done would pay off one day.

Stud's idea about Bobby was no different than the popular belief surrounding most other backup quarterbacks: pray like hell that your starter makes it through the season, and curse like hell if he doesn't.

Bobby held no bitterness toward Edmond at all. He was happy for him, actually. Edmond had a rough time growing up. His father was killed in a shootout with the Odessa police over drugs and the money that came with the trade. Edmond's mother abandoned him soon thereafter, dropping him off on his grandmother's doorstep in north Dallas without even a note. Edmond had been through all this before the age of three. Bobby grew up in an affluent part of town called Westlake, just north of Fort Worth. He was allowed to attend Trinity only because of some strings pulled by his father, Mel.

Practice shifted to the seven-on-seven portion, and that meant more watching for Bobby. Edmond was red hot that day. The ball never touched the ground during the seven-on-seven drill. It was clockwork for Edmond—see the coverage here, throw it over there. The single high safety takes the seven route away—look for the shallow cross coming in behind. The defense throws a quarters coverage at you, take the check down. Move those chains. Wait for the big strike. Edmond was seeing things clearly. Stud was salivating at the possibilities.

After twelve straight reps for Edmond, Bobby jogged onto the field to take one. His arm had gotten stiff from all the waiting. On his first throw, he one-hopped a stop route to a receiver in the right flat.

Stud shook his head and spat a chalky mouthful of tobacco onto the grass.

"What the hell are you doing, Dupree?" Stud whined. "Square your shoulders and hit the damn stop route."

Bobby didn't say anything because as a backup, he knew his place.

Stud stabbed another gum-full of dip into his mouth. "Montoya! Get in there," he said. "Maybe you can give us something. I need a competent backup quarterback."

Montoya took his one rep and threw a safe checkdown to the back. Stud wasn't really paying attention to Montoya's rep. He just acted like he was.

Edmond got back in there and took the last fifteen reps of seven-on-seven, throwing fourteen completions. The only misstep was when a receiver dropped a perfectly thrown ball.

Stud blew his whistle. "Get some water!" he yelled. "Team period up next! Ones versus ones!"

Bobby, Edmond, and Mickey trotted over to

where the water coolers were. While the rest of the team was congregating, the quarterbacks stayed to themselves. Another check mark in Edmond's column was that of leadership. He didn't spend a lot of time goofing around with the other guys. He was serious about his position on the team. Serious about getting out of Texas. Serious about buying his grandmother a home with the signing bonus of his first NFL contract.

"What do you think?" Bobby asked Edmond. "Think me or Mickey will get one rep during team period?"

Edmond wiped away the sheet of sweat that had formed on his forehead. Squinting against the sun, he squirted a stream of cold water into his mouth.

"No reason for even the *one*," Edmond retorted with joy, a pure joy from simply being on the field. "Only time you or Montoya get in this season is when we're up by thirty points in the second half."

Bobby smiled and Edmond did the same.

"Don't worry, Dupree," Edmond said with a pat

to Bobby's back. "I'll make sure there are a lot of blowouts this year so ya'll can get some reps."

It wasn't cockiness from Edmond. It was truth.

Stud blew his whistle again and brought the team back over to the fifty-yard line. First string versus first string at the end of the opening practice of the season equated to the first chance a coach gets to see what kind of team he has. To see if all the weight-lifting had an effect. To find out if all the sprints made anyone faster. To figure out if the hours logged in passing league helped the offense run more smoothly. And most important, to recognize who's tough and who's not.

"Guys!" Stud pleaded. "Don't bring anyone to the ground. I want to make that clear. Don't knock any of your teammates onto the ground. Thud only!"

The days where a team went full speed in practice were long gone. Running backs and receivers could run free at practice with their minds at ease. The only exceptions to this rule were along the offensive and defensive lines where contact was unavoidable.

Edmond got under center for the first play of team period. He lifted his left leg and stamped it back into the ground to bring the receiver in motion from left to right. He called out his signals with authority and scanned the defense before taking the snap. The clash of pads along the line rang out and reminded everyone present to recall what they loved about football in the first place: the collision, the confrontation.

The first play was a handoff to Trinity's first-string back, Tevin Marcus, a north-south runner, in the mold of Sealy, Texas great, Eric Dickerson. Tevin took the handoff and followed his pulling left guard, Degarmo, through a front-side hole. Marcus made the first defender miss and would've scored had the strong safety not come down to make a shoestring tackle. Edmond ran over to the sideline to get the next play from Stud—who also served as the Trinity's offensive coordinator—simulating the experience of getting the play call during a live game.

Edmond ran back to the huddle and looked into

his guys' eyes. Each member of the starting offense met his stare. Edmond was ready to take Trinity somewhere special, and his guys were ready to follow him to that place. The quarterback barked out the play and broke the huddle. He scanned the defense before crouching down behind center. The defense showed a basic cover-two look. Edmond knew the seam route would be open right down the middle of the defense. All he had to do was move the free safety to the left with his eyes, and the seam would open up like the Red Sea. It would be like stealing.

After the snap, Edmond took a seven-step drop and looked to his left in an attempt to fool the free safety. When the defender took the bait, Edmond snapped his head over to the middle of the field and saw his tight end running open down the seam. Exactly how he planned it.

Edmond could see things before they even happened now.

He planted his back foot and threw the ball on a rope. You have to throw the seam route in that fashion, giving your receiver a chance to make the catch and protect himself. Too much air under the ball, and your receiver gets blown up.

The sideline erupted after Edmond completed the pass to the tight end for a touchdown. Football holds the possibility of being harsh, much like life itself holds the possibility of harshness, or what some might call "cruelty." This harshness or cruelty was apparent to Stud when he looked back to where the pass was released. He didn't see a proud Edmond Daniels pointing to the sky, and then celebrating with his teammates. No. Stud saw Edmond Daniels on the ground, writhing in agony, clutching his left knee.

3

EDMOND SAT IN THE TRAINER'S ROOM WITH A towel over his head. Stud was at the end of the table with tears welled up in his eyes. Edmond cried too, but his tears were due to the physical pain. The weight of the situation hadn't sunk in yet: the loss of a promised season, the potential loss of a scholarship. In total, it was the loss of a life-long dream. Stud couldn't say anything; he simply put his hand on Edmond's right ankle and left it there. The trainer rubbed Edmond's left knee gently, searching for the unstable ligament. When the trainer's hand reached the spot right under the kneecap, Edmond thrashed. The trainer knew. Edmond knew. Stud knew.

"ACL," the trainer said.

"That's a fact?" Stud asked the trainer.

"We gotta get you to a hospital to do the MRI," the trainer said to Edmond.

And with that, the trainer tapped the damaged left knee gently.

"Will I . . . " Edmond whispered through congestion. "Will I ever play again?"

"Yes," the trainer said. "With a lot of hard work. But honestly, not this season. This season is over for you, Edmond."

Stud stood quietly in place, avoiding eye contact with Edmond and the trainer. Realizing that the star player and coach needed a moment of privacy, the trainer left the room.

"What happened?" Edmond asked. "On the play?"

"I didn't see it," Stud said. "I was looking downfield, admiring the pass you threw."

"I looked the safety off too," Edmond said,

shaking his head. "Just like you taught in the quarterbacks' room."

"Yeah."

"I'm scared, Coach."

Stud didn't respond right away because he was never good in these moments. He couldn't say that Edmond was going to be okay because he didn't really believe it. Stud could've lied to Edmond and told him that he *knew* he'd pull through and be the same player, but that wasn't Stud's style.

"I've seen a lot of kids make it back, Edmond," Stud finally said. "A lot of kids."

And that was all he had to offer his star quarterback. Edmond was all alone now. Though aided by others—trainers, teammates, his grandmother—his fate would be primarily dependent on his will alone.

"I'm gonna call your grandmother," Stud said. "She needs to know before we transport you to the hospital."

Edmond put his head down and two thick streams fell on both sides of his face.

"Tell her I'm sorry, Coach," Edmond said. "Just tell her that."

Edmond took the towel that was over his head and cried into it. Stud came close and put his arms around his quarterback.

. . . .

Bobby was waiting in Stud's office when Stud walked in from the trainer's room.

Stud sat down at his desk without realizing that Bobby was sitting right in front of him.

"Coach," Bobby said softly.

It was enough to snap Stud out of it.

"Yeah?" Stud huffed. "Oh yeah. Bobby."

"How is Edmond?"

"ACL. He's done for the year."

Bobby gulped but not out of fear of being elevated up the depth chart. The involuntary act was more a reaction to the sense of genuine loss over Edmond's injury that Bobby felt in his gut. Though they weren't good friends off the field, Edmond and Bobby got along well enough on the practice field and in the meeting room. It helped that Edmond never thought much of Bobby in terms of challenging him for the starting spot.

"Go home, Bobby," Stud said. "Go home and think about this. I sure as hell have to."

Bobby got up slowly and made his way to the door. He turned around before leaving and looked at his coach. Stud was staring straight ahead, transfixed on something that was only visible to him.

4

MEL DUPREE SAT IN HIS OFFICE AT THE DUPREE family home, smoking a Cuban cigar and staring at the phone. He wasn't staring at it because he expected a call. It was just a habit.

Bobby's father was an important businessman in north Texas and especially celebrated in Dallas. He had made his fortune in commercial real estate, and over the years as his coffers swelled, he dabbled in other arenas as well. All told, there wasn't a black-tie event in town that Mel wasn't invited to, or a construction project green-lit without him looking over the deal first. But as far as fatherhood went,

Mel wasn't quite as successful. His relationship with Bobby could be best described as tolerable.

Mel was less than thrilled with Bobby's performance—or lack thereof—on the football field, and Bobby returned the favor by not being the biggest fan of his father's many business pursuits. Mel dreamed that Bobby could make amends for his own ineffectual athletic past. Yet, with Bobby riding the pine, those hopes were nearly extinguished.

Things were even more complicated because just one month before Edmond tore up his knee, Mel had donated ten thousand dollars to Trinity High School's athletic department for brand new uniforms and practice gear. Bobby and all his teammates were in attendance at the ceremony when Mel presented a check to Trinity's athletic director. Bobby's teammates didn't understand his resentment toward his father. To them, Mel was mighty fine as a father; many of them would've killed to have a father who could broker seats in Jerry Jones's skybox during Cowboys games. His teammates would have loved to call a man like Mel "Dad."

Mel had given large sums of money before. This particular ten thousand meant something, however, because it represented Mel's first donation that went directly to Trinity's football program. The money wasn't meant as an outright bribe to conjure up more field time for Bobby, but he knew deep down the gesture couldn't hurt. Mel looked at his donation as an investment, say in case Edmond Daniels went down, and Stud needed a reminder of who the backup QB should be. For Mel, this worked much like the "investments" he made in taking prospective partners out to expensive dinners or to outings in Mr. Jones's skybox. For Bobby, the Cowboys games and "investments" on Mel's behalf were not enough; what he wanted instead was a more invested father.

Something moved in Mel's peripheral vision, and he craned his neck to eye the security feeds broadcasting on the flat-screen TV on the wall. A car pulled up to the gate that guarded the front of the Dupree house. It was Bobby's car. Mel gazed at the slightly scrambled image with something like indifference. But soon, the visual turned Mel's indifference into disgust. His only son was a benchwarmer, not *good* enough to get on the field.

The gate swung open and Bobby drove in toward the house. Mel put out his cigar and went to meet Bobby at the front door. Not because he wanted to, quite frankly, but because lately, his wife, Bobby's mother, Holly, had been harping on Mel "to try harder" with Bobby. Over the years, Mel had been an unfailing presence on the sideline the first day of practice. But with Bobby a permanent fixture on the sideline, what was the use? The door opened and Bobby walked in, still stunned by the events at practice and the ascension up the depth chart afterwards.

"Hey son," Mel said, monotonously. "How'd it go out there today?"

"It went . . . "

Bobby's demeanor was peculiar in a way that was

somehow uneven; something that was totally against Bobby's flatlining nature. This piqued Mel's interest.

"What's up, Bobby?" Mel asked, making eye contact with his son and drumming up as much sincerity as he had.

"Edmond," Bobby said. "Edmond tore up his knee at the end of practice."

Mel leaned in close. "Is that right?"

"Yeah, I guess, I'm the starter," Bobby said, not believing the words, just saying them.

A grin curled onto Mel's face. "Now son, that's just great. That's really . . . " Mel turned away from Bobby and pumped his fists and clapped his hands. " . . . really fantastic news!"

Bobby was startled by his father's reaction to Edmond's injury. Though he knew his father loved football, he had never seen Mel react like this. Mel, not one to be tone-deaf, realized that his reaction to Edmond's unfortunate injury was inappropriate. He gathered himself and put a diplomatic hand on Bobby's shoulder.

"That's awful news about Edmond," Mel said. "We'll be sure to pray for him. And I'll personally see to it that he gets the best medical care that Dallas has to offer."

"I'm gonna go up to my room," Bobby said, overwhelmed from the sheer weight of his day. The violent swing from backup to starter still had not set in. "Coach told me to think about my opportunity."

Mel grabbed his son by both shoulders now. He knew how to be decent, but this was big. "Stud said that?" Mel pulled Bobby close. "What else did he say? You are the starter now? They aren't gonna go with that little snot-nose Montoya are they?"

Bobby strained to put distance between he and his father. Mel eyed him suspiciously, and wouldn't let go of his son until he got the answer he wanted.

"No," Bobby said. "I'm the starter now."

"Well hot damn!" Mel screamed, damning diplomacy, decency, and anything else that clashed with the laws of football. "This is great news, Bobby! We gotta tell your mother! Holly!"

Mel turned his head and called out into the vast space of the Dupree house, "Holly! Get your butt over here! Bobby has news!"

He turned back to Bobby.

"We have to celebrate!"

"I'm gonna go up to my room to think," Bobby said, shedding himself from his father's arms.

"You go do that, son!" Mel said. "And when you're ready, come on down for dinner, and you, me, your mom, and your sister—we'll all celebrate."

Bobby went up to his room, shut the door, and lay down in bed with headphones over his ears. He wasn't that big into music, but needed it to drown out the sound of his father's hollering.

· ·

It didn't take Mel long to pick up the phone and share the news with everyone he knew. The Trinity boosters, with whom he shared beers and one too many whiskies at the country club, were the first to know. These loyal Trinity followers were sad initially—sad that Edmond was lost for the season. But by the end of the calls Mel had sold each and every one of them on his son. Mel could sell anything really. The next calls were to Mel's parents, Bobby's grandparents. They had never come to watch their grandson play football. Not in pee-wee. Not in Pop Warner. That would change. Bobby was the *man* now. It was his team now. The whole season, which had rested on Edmond's wide and chiseled shoulders, now rested on Bobby's narrow ones. Mel could hardly believe it.

Prior to this, Mel had come pretty close to losing all hope for his son. What's the point of being on the team if you ain't gonna get on the field? Mel could never understand what drove Bobby to keep playing, despite not being on the field. Mel Dupree never settled for second best. And here was his son, his only son, riding the bench. Well, those days were done. According to Mel, every young man needed a turning point in his life. Like when he was in his early twenties, fresh out of SMU, without a pot to piss in, and turned his first deal for profit. Maybe this moment was Bobby's turning point?

When Bobby finally came out of his room and padded down the stairs, it was well past dinner. His mom and sister were in their rooms. Only Mel was still around, sitting in the family's spacious kitchen, with a bottle of Old Grandad and an Alamo beer. Mel tipped the beer to his son and it nearly sloshed out through its bottleneck. Bobby had hoped that Mel would be asleep by now, but should have known better.

"Done thinkin', son?" Mel asked.

"I guess."

"Well get yourself something to eat and have a glass of milk. You need good bones for all the hits you're gonna take."

Bobby hadn't even pondered the football part yet. He had spent the time in his room thinking about Edmond and all *he* had lost. Bobby felt genuine sorrow at Edmond's plight. Now, here in the kitchen with his dad, Bobby got around to acknowledging the opportunity that was before him. The opportunity to be on the field, leading the team. This excited him, also in a genuine way, though he didn't have the knowledge or the experience of showing outward confidence.

"I think," Mel said, before taking a shot of Old Grandad, "this is gonna be a hell of a season."

Bobby grabbed the ingredients to make a sandwich out of the refrigerator. Under the usual circumstances, Bobby often acted as if Mel wasn't there, even when his father was an arm's-length away or within earshot. But these weren't the usual circumstances. Bobby was the starter now.

"Aren't you just about as fired up as you've ever been?"

"I'm looking forward to playing," Bobby said, "but it sucks for Edmond."

"Now, Bobby, I know what Edmond is going through . . . is rough. But you can't think about that now. You gotta take this thing by the horns and goddamnit, you gotta squeeze it."

Bobby finished making a sandwich and replaced the items in the fridge. He hip-checked the door closed and looked at the kitchen doorway. Bobby wanted nothing more than to bolt up to his room and eat his sandwich in peace.

"Sit with your old man, son," Mel said.

Bobby walked over without enthusiasm. Mel was too many drinks in to notice. And besides, nothing was going to ruin this moment for Mel.

"When you're out there, you gotta look alive. No more holding a clipboard. No more backwards cap. You're the one now. And when the guys with Trinity across their chests look into your eyes, well, they got to know it. They got to know that you're the one."

This one-sided conversation that Mel had coerced Bobby into, was uncomfortable now. Maybe it was due to the fact that Mel hadn't said more than two words to Bobby in the last week or so. Or perhaps it was because two weeks earlier, Mel told Bobby that this was the season that he'd stop making it a priority to be at all of Bobby's games, that his weekend business trips would take precedence over watching Bobby stand on the sidelines.

"I want you to say it, Bobby," Mel said, before taking one last shot of whisky.

Bobby watched as the liquor ran like a river down his father's throat. He wished that the liquor would somehow make his father stop talking. But the opposite always seemed to be true.

"You're not gonna think about Edmond anymore, Bobby," Mel said. "That's enough."

Bobby picked at his sandwich. His appetite, spoiled.

"I want to hear you say it," Mel said, at a low growl now. "I want to hear you say, 'I'm the one.'"

Bobby could almost hear the sound of his heart beating. It was late and the Dupree house was a cavern that swallowed up sound. This first dose of pressure came from Mel. Up to that point, Bobby had felt none. This was pressure that Bobby did not need. He hadn't even set foot on the field.

Mel eyed his son with the persistent glare that was talked about in every boardroom all across north Texas. It wouldn't relent until Bobby gave in.

"I'm the one," Bobby said with no emotion. Then he took a huge bite of his sandwich and dry-gulped it down.

5

STUD DIDN'T SAY ANYTHING TO BOBBY BEFORE practice the next morning because he was still in shock about Edmond. He also thought that Bobby was fragile and didn't want to rattle his backup QB further. Stud was detached from the team as a whole, really. Bobby noticed all of this. *So much for the head coach-starting quarterback bond,* he thought. Bobby stuck with the quarterback's coach, Pete Bohannon, instead.

"It's real simple, Bobby," Pete said. "We're gonna practice a lot of different plays. But we're also gonna scale the offense back some. It's not realistic to expect you to handle the entire playbook after not playing for . . . "

Pete eyes narrowed. "How long has it been since you've started a game at quarterback?" he asked.

Bobby smiled in that way he did when he was embarrassed.

"Pee-wee," Bobby said. "Seventy-pound weight class. And that wasn't even the whole season."

"Damn, Bobby," Pete said, stuffing tobacco into his bottom lip. "Why didn't you change positions all these years?"

"I don't know," Bobby said. "I've always been a quarterback."

Pete jabbed at Bobby's shoulder pads, the spot right over his heart. He walked away from Bobby and over to Stud. There were still fifteen minutes before practice started—the team's first with Bobby at the helm. Bobby looked over to one of the team helpers, Jackson Newheart, a scrawny type that loved football but never had the size to play. Jackson was handling a football and gave Bobby eye contact.

Bobby showed Jackson his hands and he threw the ball over to him. Bobby held the ball in his hands, squeezing it at certain points, looking for the *right* feel. He always threw a "catchable" ball. That's what his coaches always said about him anyway. "Bobby would never be mistaken for having a cannon for an arm, but boy, did he throw a catchable ball. Soft, like a mouse pissing on cotton," they'd say.

All of the catchable throws that Bobby had delivered over the years did nothing to get him in the *game*. Bobby was missing something in the eyes of every one of his coaches. So one by one, season by season, he was passed over and found himself on the bench. Maybe he never wanted it enough? Whatever it had been in the past, Bobby felt like he was going to seize this *now*. He was tired of being on the bench.

Bobby nodded to Jackson, this time inviting him over to warm up his arm. None of the receivers would stand next to Bobby before practice, perhaps out of grief for losing Edmond. Mickey Montoya was pouting, like the underclassman he was, in the opposite end zone. One thing was clear: Bobby would have to win his teammates over. There would be no blind acceptance of Bobby, simply because he was "the next man up." Bobby gritted his teeth and spun his first few throws to Jackson: tight spirals that cut the thick and downtrodden humidity hanging over the field, and to a greater extent, the entire Trinity team. Jackson shook the pain out of his hands each time Bobby threw a pass to him. Bobby felt good about how he was spinning it that day—a quarterback's dream.

. . . .

The quarterback drills were a little less crowded and a lot less one-sided during the first practice after Edmond's injury. The first drill was the quarterback-center exchange. Here, Bobby got a chance to practice barking his snap count and experiment with rhythm and cadence. He was surprised by how he sounded at first. He sounded confident. He sounded like a man. There were a couple of fumbles during the drill. Bobby understood the importance of ball security just by observing Stud's nervous gesticulations as he watched the routine drill. Bobby knew there was nothing that would plant him right back on the bench faster than fumbled snaps, so he made sure to finish the drill in a clean fashion. Stud was satisfied and blew the whistle for a period change.

The wide receivers were invited over for the next drill. It was time to throw routes on "air." This drill presented a chance for the quarterback and receivers to connect without any defenders present. It was a simple way to create rhythm amongst the QBs and receivers. The ball was still jumping out of Bobby's hand. His live arm caught his receivers off guard. They were used to Bobby and his "catchable" balls. But they weren't used to this much zip. Neither was Bobby.

Stud blew his whistle.

"Okay!" he yelled. "That's enough of working the front-side throws! Let's see the back-side ones, Dupree!"

Those were the first words that Stud had said to Bobby that morning, and they were bestowed in front of the entire offense. Bobby didn't care though. He was busy now. He didn't have time to ponder his coach's apparent lack of confidence in him, nor did he have time to mill over any perceived slights. Maybe his father was right. The time for thought was over. The thoughts of Edmond were driven away with each strike Bobby threw to a streaking wide receiver.

"Boy's got some pop in his arm," Pete said. "Damn."

"These are back side throws too," Stud said. "Opposite hash. Who knew?" There was no glimmer in Stud's eye as he spoke. Even with the backhanded compliment, there was still too much shock and pain from the loss of Edmond.

"What are we gonna do, Pete?" Stud asked, as another of Bobby's throws zipped by them.

"What do you mean?" Pete replied.

"I mean, how do we come back from this?"

"Truth is we probably won't," Pete said. But there was no sadness or bitterness in Pete's voice. "Edmond was special. Our defense is good. So we'll probably be in most games."

Bobby threw another dart. This time, a deep comeback. A throw that even Edmond had trouble getting enough mustard on.

"But that's what's unique about this whole deal," Pete said, before spitting a mouthful of tobacco juice onto the field.

"What?" Stud asked.

"Gettin' Dupree ready," Pete said. "It's gonna be fun."

6

"**Y**OU KNOW I LOVE YOU, DUPREE," SAID TYRONE Gilliam, Trinity's star Senior cornerback, during the water break. "But I'm gettin' me a couple of picks off you during one-on-ones."

Bobby smiled without response. Just happy to finally be a part of it all. The trash talk he had once only observed from his annual spot on the bench was fun, even though it was one-sided at this point. Bobby hoped that with solid play, he could actually do some talking himself.

A whistle blew and it was time for one-on-ones, with wide receivers versus cornerbacks. This was always one of the livelier periods of practice, simply because of all the talent the team had at those positions. With Bobby's past, his one-on-one reps were too few and far between to judge. No one really knew what he could do. The first rep belonged to Trinity's top receiver from the year before, Brian Bell. And he was going up against Tyrone Gilliam.

Brian was a physical specimen *and* knew how to play the game. Growing up in North Dallas, he was one of those players at Pop Warner practice whom all the other kids tried to avoid during hitting drills. Now at Trinity, Brian stood six foot three, and was two hundred pounds of steel. He ran a four-five forty—forty yards in 4.5 seconds—and possessed a vertical leap of forty inches.

The player across from Brian during the first one-on-one rep wasn't afraid, however. Tyrone Gilliam was a master in his own right. A late bloomer. Not the dominant, physical freak that Brian was, Tyrone was the son of a coach who learned to play the game from the neck up at the early stages of nascency.

When a growth spurt finally arrived, Tyrone became a wizard on the football field. If he wasn't able to predict the route from film study or watching the quarterback's drop, he'd simply read the quarterback's eyes and jump the route. If a zone defense was called, Tyrone could sink right into the perfect spot for an interception, and if it was man-to-man press, he'd jam the receiver with enough force that the route would never materialize. When Tyrone was a junior, Trinity's opponents rarely threw to his side of the field. As a senior, with another off-season to sharpen his mind and body, the proposition of completing balls to his side would be iffy at best.

Bobby was just happy to be a part of this as he was usually relegated to throwing to third stringers during this portion of practice. Tyrone lined up right in front of Brian. Both of them knew what the first route was. One-on-ones always started with the "nine" route. There was no mystery. No deception. No set up. Brian was going to try to run straight by Tyrone to make a long catch, and Tyrone was going to try to jam Brian on the line of scrimmage to stop said long catch from happening. Bobby patted the ball once and called "hike!" Tyrone was too aggressive on the line and missed the jam. Brian got a clean release, and as a result, created five yards of separation. Bobby, cautious of Tyrone's make-up speed, put the ball up in the air, out in front of Brian. He didn't want to under throw his receiver and allow Tyrone to come up with the interception. In the quarterbacks' meeting room at Trinity, they were taught that it was best to overthrow Brian because there was always a chance that he could use his speed to make the catch. And one place Bobby *did* excel was the meeting room. Brian looked up in the air, and the sun blinded him for a millisecond. He blinked and located the ball as it dropped into his hands. Bobby's pass was right in stride. Brian sprinted into the end zone. Tyrone dropped his head. Brian made everyone look mediocre—even other great players. But none of it would have been possible without Bobby's accurate throw.

"Atta boy, Dupree!" Pete shouted from behind the drill.

Stud looked on. He wasn't yet a believer. Any person could throw routes without a live defense coming to take to their head off. Stud needed more evidence to believe in Bobby Dupree.

Brian didn't celebrate his triumph over Tyrone. He wasn't the type to boast—never at practice. And especially not at a teammate's expense. Tyrone was the strong, silent type as well, man enough to give a pat to Brian's helmet before running back over to the line of scrimmage. Brian and Tyrone had a quiet respect for each other. As seniors, they were two leaders on a team that needed leadership, particularly after its star quarterback was knocked out for the year. The two didn't socialize much out of school. They came from different backgrounds. Tyrone's father played a large role in his son's life, while Brian never knew his.

"Nice throw," Brian said to Bobby, as he ran to the back of the receiver line.

"Thanks," Bobby said.

The next receiver jumped up to the line of scrimmage and the next corner did the same. Tyrone, however, did not run to the back of the defensive backs' line. Bobby waited as the two DBs hashed out who would take the next rep.

"I need to make up for that weak-ass rep!" Tyrone called out to no one in particular.

Because Tyrone was who he was within Trinity's pecking order, he could do what he pleased. The other cornerback, who was at the head of the line and whose turn it rightly was, had to wait until Tyrone was satisfied with his performance.

Bobby called out, "Hike!" This time, Tyrone got a healthy jam on the line, and when the receiver finally got into his route, Tyrone was running with him stride for stride. Bobby lofted the pass up and hoped for the best.

Tyrone batted the pass down and ran to the back of the line, shaking his head. Even though his second rep was successful, getting burned by Brian on the first one gnawed at him. Tyrone wanted to succeed against the best, and Brian represented the best in his eyes. Bobby, for his part, realized that when Brian was the one running the routes, there was a larger margin of error than with the other receivers. *No wonder Edmond looked so good throwing to Brian,* he thought.

By the end of one-on-one drills, Bobby's arm was sore. Not that he would let anybody know it; he was having too much fun.

Bobby kept his mouth shut because it was time to bring the whole team together and end practice with a scrimmage, with ones versus ones, to see where the team's frontline players were after experiencing the bumps and bruises of two practices. This would be Bobby's first chance to receive the play, get in the huddle, look in all his guys' eyes, and take a snap as the starting quarterback of Trinity. Stud still wasn't himself. Though Bobby had been near flawless during his first practice as starter, Stud hadn't seen enough to anoint Bobby a savior. He was determined to observe Bobby and make judgements later. Pete was the one who took a hands-on approach with Bobby.

"Okay, Bobby," Pete said. "Let's go Zebra, I-right, 92 power."

Bobby nodded and ran over to the huddle. He wedged himself in and knelt down in front of the guys. His guys.

"Okay," Bobby said. "Zebra, I-right, 92 power on two, on two. Ready break!"

A chorus of claps rang out as the offensive line approached the line of scrimmage.

Bobby looked out at the defense. He never dreamed he'd get this chance. The rush of being on the field made Bobby determined to keep his eyes open, for he did not want to miss a thing. Not a snap. Not a passing interaction with a teammate. Edmond getting injured on the football field was a plausible outcome. Players were injured all the time while playing football. But Edmond's durability and sheer star power were two forces that made Bobby feel like he would always be relegated to the bench.

He got down under center and called out his cadence with a confidence that was growing.

"Blue, thirty-two! Blue, thirty-two!"

The defensive line twitched with anticipation. The strong safety spotted something and crept down into the box.

Bobby didn't notice any of the details. He could only perceive the entire landscape now. He lifted his right leg and put Brian in motion.

"Blue, thirty-two! Blue, thirty-two! Set hut! Hut!"

The center snapped the ball and then there was thunder. Pads exploded against one another during the basic, up-the-gut running play. Bobby handed the ball off to Tevin, and as soon as he crossed the line of scrimmage, the strong safety leveled him from the side, extracting a gasp from the running back and a collective "ooh" from the sideline. Back on the field, the defensive players whooped like wild, mad children, and this was just the opening play of the scrimmage. An offensive lineman helped Tevin up off the field, and the running back rubbed his tender ribs. Tevin glared at Bobby before Bobby ran over to the sideline to get the next play from Pete.

"What happened there?" Pete asked.

Bobby looked back out to the field and then at Pete.

"We gained a yard," Bobby said.

"And?"

Bobby didn't know what Pete was getting at but was smart enough to know that Tevin's nasty look meant something.

"An eighth man dropped into the box—the strong safety," Pete said. "Now I know you haven't played in a hell of a long time. But I also know that you've been to every quarterback meeting in the past two seasons. What do we do if the eighth man drops into the box and the defense shows a single high-safety look?"

With the priming, Bobby was able to conjure the answer to Pete's quiz question.

"If they commit an eighth guy in the box," Bobby said, "I have the freedom to change the play to a throw."

Pete nodded. "And what determines whether or not you check to pass?"

"Down and distance. Time and score," Bobby said.

Pete patted the back of Bobby's helmet. "Goddamn you do have some brains up there. Now you have to use 'em."

Bobby had had the information stored somewhere in his head. But a player having the information in his head is one thing. Calling on that information and executing in real time is another.

"I told you earlier," Pete said. "We're gonna trust you. We're not gonna hamstring you with predictable play calls once you get comfortable with the basic actions of being out on the field. By the time the season comes, you'll *know* most of the offense. More than enough to be functional. You just gotta let it fly when you're out there. I'm confident in you. Your job is to play with confidence."

Bobby met Pete's eyes.

"Good?" Pete asked.

Bobby nodded.

"Okay, let's go kings, sixty smoke, ninety-four stack," Pete said. "As always, look for Brian first on the dig, and if he's covered up, work backside and look for Branch on the curl."

Bobby raised his hand in the air. "Kings! Kings!"

Tevin and the fullback, Evan Suarez left the field. Two receivers trotted onto the field and took their places in the huddle. Bobby joined in and called the play. Brian lined up to the far left in the X position with another wideout to his right in the slot. The right side of the formation had the same setup, except for a tight end that was lined up in a three-point stance next the right tackle.

Bobby looked over the defense. Two safeties in the middle of the field—the hallmark of a cover-two defense. Bobby knew that if Brian got a clean release, the dig would be open. He got down under center and looked to his left. Brian shot him a glance of recognition. He too, recognized the cover-two shell.

"Blue, thirty-two! Blue, thirty-two! Set hut!"

Bobby took the snap and then a five-step drop. Brian got the clean release that Bobby had anticipated, and by the time he, Brian, reached his seventeen-yard landmark and stuck his foot in the ground for the in-cut, Bobby released the pass. The ball whistled by the outside linebacker's ear-hole, as the defender buzzed into the curl area, and hit Brian in stride. Brian split the two safeties and raced into the end zone. Trinity's senior center, Corey Meredith, picked Bobby up and pointed him skyward like a religious idol. The sideline erupted. Bobby's offensive teammates turned to him with wide eyes. The caution was out of them. Their eyes seemed to offer an acceptance of Bobby into the fold. He was one of them now.

Brian ran straight over to Bobby after the TD and slapped him a high-five. Trinity's defenders, on the other hand, didn't know what hit them. They couldn't conceive that a player who looked like Bobby, a player with no pedigree to speak of, could throw a ball like *that*.

"Hot damn!" Pete gushed to Stud. "See that? On a dig? Hardest route to throw in football. You got a QB that can throw the deep dig, you damn sure got a chance."

Stud had finally seen enough. A quarterback doesn't simply walk onto the field, get lucky and complete a dig route into a tight window. It took Edmond half a season to be able to throw the dig route on time, and with that kind of precision and accuracy. It took Stud himself forever to throw a decent dig route when he was Trinity's quarterback fifteen years before. But Bobby shot it in there on his first attempt. Against Trinity's number one defense. Bobby saw the defense. He saw Brian. And he threw the ball with anticipation, pace and without fear.

Stud knew what he had to do now.

After practice Bobby's body was sore all over. It wasn't just about his arm anymore. He had to listen and answer to his entire body now. Mentally, Bobby was in a good place. Stud didn't say much to the team after, except that Edmond was going in for surgery soon and that he'd like the guys to go visit him at the hospital. Stud dismissed the team, and little by little, the players made their way off the field and into the locker room.

Even though the school year hadn't begun yet, there was a group of girls congregated in the bleachers after practice, and it wasn't just any group of girls. These girls had status inside the walls of Trinity High School. The group was made of individuals who were the girlfriends or prospective girlfriends of the players on the team. All of the players who saw regular time on the field had at least one girl. Bobby, on the other hand, was a backup in this department as well.

When Bobby walked past the bleachers on his way to the locker room, he locked eyes with Larissa Mumphrey. Larissa caught Bobby's gaze and quickly looked away. Inexperienced with girls as he was, Bobby put his head down and hustled into the locker room. He had always had a thing for Larissa, ever since the first day of school in the sixth grade, when he saw her for the first time during P.E., in her gym uniform. He'd go home at night and dream about Larissa's powerful thighs poking out of her gym shorts. But when he crossed paths with her in school, he'd do and say nothing of substance. Years went by with Bobby suffering in silence.

Larissa was an athlete too. She ran on the cross-country team at Trinity, and this tenuous athletic link between she and Bobby served as the basis for their crossed paths over the years. Other than the occasional awkward and uneasy encounter at an athletic banquet or fundraising event, the truth was,

Larissa didn't know much about Bobby, let alone the fact that he had a major crush on her.

7

"**S**IT DOWN, BOBBY," STUD SAID IN HIS OFFICE, thirty minutes after practice had ended.

Bobby's right shoulder was wrapped in ice and he still reeked of sweat as he hadn't gotten the chance to shower yet. Pete had snapped him up right after practice because he wanted to go over some coverage stuff in the quarterbacks' room even as the trainer looked over his sore shoulder after practice. Bobby went right to Stud's office after finishing with Pete. He was quickly becoming accustomed to the life of a starting quarterback.

"You did a good job today," Stud said.

"I'll get used to all the checks," Bobby said, ignoring Stud's compliment, with the hope that Stud would recognize his unwillingness to let praise get to his head. "I missed that one with the loaded box."

"It'll come," Stud said.

And then the two of them were silent. They weren't used to spending time talking with one another. Just a few passing words here and there. Stud was uncomfortable because of what he was about to tell Bobby. The shock of losing Edmond had finally begun to wear off—mostly because of Bobby's unexpected competence during his first practice—and if Trinity was to have any chance at success during the season, Stud had to give his new starting quarterback a vote of confidence. Up until Bobby threw the dig route in practice, Stud had no hopes for the season. The dig route changed everything.

"This is your team now," Stud said. "We're not going to go anywhere this season unless you lead us there." He paused. "And I believe in you."

Bobby was stunned, though he had the presence of mind to hide the giddiness strewn about his insides.

"Thanks, Coach."

"You're off to a good start," Stud said. "That dig route you threw to Brian . . . " He whistled. "That was a beauty."

"Yeah," Bobby said. "It felt good coming out of my hand. I was . . . I don't know. I was really seeing things good out there today."

"Good."

Stud nodded as if Bobby would say the next word, but it never came. Just more silence.

"How's your dad, Bobby?" Stud asked.

Stud knew Mel Dupree's importance in terms of his generosity. He also knew that now that Bobby was the starting quarterback, he would probably be seeing a lot more of Mel.

"I mean, how is he handling this news of your promotion?" Stud asked.

"He's happy," Bobby said, flexing his right shoulder to test its range of motion.

"I didn't see him out there."

"He's in San Antonio on business," Bobby said. "He'll be back tonight. He'll probably come to practice tomorrow."

There was that silence again. Bobby hoped that Stud didn't purport his silence to be a sign that Mel's attention would be a pressure-filled distraction. Stud was somewhere in that ballpark with his thinking as he knew all too well the pressure a rabid football dad, driven by a vicarious vision, could exert on a son. Stud had experienced the tension firsthand with his own overbearing father when he was the starter at Trinity. He crossed his fingers that Mel Dupree wouldn't become a problem.

"Make sure you ice up regularly," Stud said with a nod to Bobby's shoulder. "And get some rest. You have responsibilities to people other than yourself now. The team relies on you. So be smart."

Bobby nodded. Stud's words had sunk in

straightaway. There was no need for additional reflection. This wasn't just about a game anymore. It surely hadn't felt like that out on the practice field.

8

THE FIRST DAY OF SCHOOL USUALLY DIDN'T MEAN much to Bobby, but this time everything was loaded. Every glance, whisper, and smile was ripe with something deeper. The girls, who up until that point had little idea that Bobby Dupree existed, were also coming out of the woodwork in droves. They now regarded Bobby with a newfound curiosity. This strange attention made Bobby feel uncomfortable for the most part, though he wished that his celebrity status would cause Larissa to give him a little attention.

Football meant so much to seemingly everyone at

Trinity—not just the players. Each school year, the mood within the halls swayed with the results of the team. This season was supposed to be a memorable one with Edmond as quarterback. It was supposed to be the season that ended at Cowboys Stadium, site of the Texas High School Championships, and home to the Dallas Cowboys. But the people in the halls weren't so sure now. They looked at Bobby as people do at some brand-new, unknown object. He was shiny but foreign. The trust was not there in his ability, yet his position as the starting quarterback gave the student body pause. They now gawked each time he passed by, whereas before he could travel the halls freely, without inciting reaction. No one knew what he was capable of. Bobby himself didn't know. One thing the people at Trinity were sure of was that Bobby was not as good as Edmond Daniels. They would not swallow that hopeful promise without any evidence to the contrary.

"Hi Bobby," said a well-developed, blonde ninth grader, whom Bobby didn't know, as they passed by one another in the hallway.

"Hello," Bobby replied.

She giggled and scurried along toward her friends.

He stopped at his locker, opened it up, and took a deep breath into it. By the time he had gathered his books, closed his locker and turned around, Larissa was walking by on her way to class. Bobby thought about turning around to face his locker, but a blunder like that would give off the vibe of insanity because his locker was closed. Instead, he did something out of character.

"Hi Larissa," Bobby said.

She looked up and seemed to smile out of reflex. Larissa remembered Bobby's stare as he ran off the field after practice.

"I'm Bobby—"

"I know who you are."

"Oh," Bobby said.

"You're the starting quarterback now, aren't you?"

"Yeah, it sucks what happened to Edmond," Bobby said.

Larissa didn't respond to that because she didn't know Edmond, nor did she aspire to. In fact, she was different than the rest of the students at Trinity, in the sense that she didn't care at all about football.

"I saw you out there after practice the other day," Bobby said.

She sighed. "Yeah, my friend McKenzie is seeing one of the guys on the team, and she begged me to come with her."

"You mean you don't have a boyfriend on the team?"

"I don't date football players."

The words didn't bother Bobby. For some reason, they made him like Larissa even more. Maybe it was because up until recently, he wasn't a football player, and this brief moonlighting as one would be a simple cameo. Whatever it took to know Larissa, Bobby was up for. Her raven hair and dark eyes stood out at Trinity, where most of the girls who followed the team were blonde with blue eyes. Her words highlighted the contrast that much more.

"Well, I gotta get to class," she said.

"Okay," Bobby said. "Maybe I'll see you around."

"Yeah," she said, before turning around and walking away. She thought that Bobby was nice, and that there was something different about him, but then quickly threw water on the thought. *After all, he is a football player, and football players aren't to be trusted*, she thought.

. . . .

That day after school, Bobby went to practice with a spring in his step. Larissa Mumphrey knew who he was.

"Yo, Bobby," called out Mike Goldson, a senior offensive tackle who manned the right side. "How do you like actually being known at school now?"

"How'd you know?" Bobby asked with narrowed eyes.

"It happened to all of us," Mike said with a sweeping hand gesture around the field. "Once you start, that's when the attention comes. It's kind of funny to me. It's not like I'm out here doing this for any of them. My only priority is to get a scholarship and get my ass into college. I couldn't care less about all these people at school, living and dying off what we do out here."

"I don't care either," Bobby said. "I'm just trying to do my best."

"Cool," Mike said. "Keep it that way. Don't let any of the other stuff mess you up."

Practice started with an emphasis on upping the tempo. Now that Bobby had shown that he could function, the pace would be increased to mimic the chaotic nature of a real game. The team jumped from drill to drill without instruction from the coaches. This was a veteran team that knew where it wanted to go. The injury to Edmond was a bump in the road, a substantial bump given how talented he was, but Bobby showed that he was able to manage the offense and that fact mattered within the locker room. Once the guys realized that Bobby was not a liability, they decided that they'd put it on the line for him. Edmond was no longer with them. Cold as it was, the team had no choice but to move on from its grief.

"Yeah!" Pete and Stud cried in unison after Bobby fired a third down strike to Brian early in the scrimmage. The affair was being dominated by Bobby and the rest of first team offense. The entire practice up to that point was a flawless exercise for Bobby. Only two of his passes hit the ground and one of them was dropped on an accurate throw.

Stud blew his whistle and called for a ball from Jackson, the team helper. Stud placed the ball on the fifty-yard line, right in the center of the field.

"Listen up!" Stud said. "We're gonna simulate a late game situation! Offense is down by four points with a minute thirty left on the clock. No timeouts. Touchdown wins the game."

The defense hooted and hollered as it took its

place on one side of the fifty. Bobby ran over to Pete to get the first play. Pete looked over his play list with a pregnant bulge in his bottom lip. Bobby could smell the tobacco that was sunbaked onto Pete's lower lip.

"Alright," Pete said. "When we have no timeouts, remember that you're always looking to get the ball to the sideline. But the defense knows that too. So make sure any throw outside the numbers is a safe one. Or as a last resort, throw it in the middle of the field and hustle the guys up to the line to kill the clock for the next play."

Bobby nodded.

"No sacks," Pete said before spitting a brown globule onto the field. "Sacks are killers."

"No sacks," Bobby repeated.

"Let's go posse, Roger, nine-ninety-five," Pete said. "Work strong-side first, then out to Brian. If you get a strong-side blitz, the slot knows to go hot and break off his route. And you have your back in the flat as an outlet if all else fails."

Bobby's head was swimming. It was almost too much to think about. He needed to see it on the field. See it and react.

"Got it?" Pete asked.

Bobby nodded and ran to the huddle.

He knelt down in front of his guys. It was quiet inside the circle. Everyone's eyes were on him. He looked around before speaking the play. Bobby wasn't used to this kind of responsibility and certainly not used to mattering this much. He didn't want to let this feeling go.

"Alright guys," Bobby said. "Posse, Roger, nine-ninety-five on two. If we get a strong side blitz, I'm coming hot to you, Devin. Make sure you break it off and show me your eyes."

Devin Williams, Trinity's diminutive jitterbug of a slot receiver, nodded and placed his mouthpiece between his teeth.

"Break!"

Bobby got to the line and scanned the defense. The initial look resembled zone coverage. Bobby looked to his right and locked eyes with Brian. The cornerback in front of him, Tyrone, was off seven yards. Bobby then looked to his left and the cornerback over there was aligned the same way. Both of the safeties were deep. It *was* zone. Bobby knelt down under the center.

"Blue thirty-two, blue thirty-two, set hut, hut!"

He took the snap and dropped back to pass. No blitz. The strong side linebacker carried Devin up the seam, and the safety on that side covered Brian too. There was nowhere to throw on the right side, except to the running back, Tevin, in the flat. As soon as Bobby's back foot hit seven steps, he let the pass go to Tevin.

The back caught the pass and made the first defender miss. Tevin tried to get out of bounds to stop the clock, but was tackled inbounds. The play gained twelve yards. As the clock ran, Bobby hustled the offense to the line of scrimmage and got it set. He made sure that the formation was legal before snapping the ball. In a real game, an illegal formation penalty under two minutes with no timeouts would be a killer because of the ten-second runoff.

Bobby snapped the ball and killed the clock. It was second and ten with a minute and three seconds left on the clock. Trinity needed thirty-eight yards to win the "game."

The call of "Kings! Kings!" rang out from the sideline. A fourth receiver ran into the huddle and took Tevin's place in the formation.

The new receiver relayed the next two plays to Bobby, and Bobby relayed that info to rest of the huddle. Trinity's offense got to the line of scrimmage, armed with the two plays. The offensive lineman called out their responsibilities as Bobby eyed the defense, searching for a tip. This time the defense showed pressure.

Bobby took the snap and pressure came off both edges in the form of blitzing outside linebackers. On his drop, Bobby felt one of the linebackers bearing in on him to his right. Instinctively, he made a spin move and escaped out of the pocket to the left. Bobby couldn't differentiate his offensive teammates from the defenders. All he saw were flashes. He decided to tuck the ball away and run. Bobby was no Edmond Daniels when it came to using his feet. But something was changing in him. Where he was known before as slow, Bobby was now deceptively quick. The confidence of being on the field had taken hold of him and morphed him into something he was not.

With a series of body fakes, he made two defenders miss. Twenty yards later, an oncoming defender in pursuit leveled Bobby from the side, right in his ribs. The hit took all the air out of him. Even worse, he was tackled in the field of play, allowing the clock to run. Bobby tried to breathe but there was no available air in his lungs. The ball was set at the eighteen-yard line and the clock ticked: forty, thirty-nine, thirty-eight. Mike Goldson scraped Bobby up off the field and set him on his feet. The moment he tried to steady himself was when the dizziness struck. Though his torso took the brunt, the sheer force of the collision affected his head as well. Bobby could barely keep himself upright but had no choice but to. No matter how it materialized, he had to lead his team to a touchdown.

He looked over to the sideline and perceived Pete and Stud shooting blurry hand signals that held no meaning to him and his woozy state. Bobby shook his head, knocked the cobwebs loose, and finally, his vision returned along with the air in his lungs. He pivoted, believing he was on his way to the huddle. Wrong, he was on his way to the sideline instead.

Brian Bell grabbed him by the collar and steered him in the right direction. Bobby tried again to look over to the sideline and still could not make out the signs and sounds coming from it.

"Aw, forget it," Bobby grumbled. His teammates were translating the signals from the sideline but Bobby ignored them all.

"Okay," he said, to the loose huddle that surrounded him. "We got Kings . . ." Bobby finger-counted the four receivers in the huddle.

"Let's go Kings, nine-ninety-nine," he said. "All seams."

The rest of the offense was quiet in the huddle as was the sideline. Bobby looked up to the scoreboard and there were fifteen seconds left in counting. The offense broke the huddle. It was clear that Bobby did not get the right play in. But there was nothing to be done now. In a real game, Stud would have had no choice but to rely on his quarterback to make the right call. That sort of helplessness would have crushed him. But here in practice, a fortuitous gem of a late-game situation had presented itself. Stud bent over and put both hands on his knees. He studied Bobby. He needed to find out if the pressure would break his new starting quarterback.

Bobby hurried under center and yelled, "Go!"

He took the snap and dropped seven steps, stumbling on the seventh step as the pass rush converged on him. Bobby recognized that Brian had a step on Tyrone, but with safety help over the top. There was no time to look elsewhere. Bobby patted the ball once and let it fly. A defensive tackle drilled him right in the chest as he released the pass. The ball stayed up in the air for what seemed like an eternity. Brian Bell tried to gauge where it would land; the very back corner of the end zone, he estimated. Brian stole a glance at the hard-charging safety. Brian ran as fast as he could. He wanted to catch *this* pass, not only for himself, but also for Bobby Dupree. He stretched out both arms as far as they would go. The ball stuck to his hands like a fly in molasses, and as the safety torpedoed into him, he gripped the ball.

Touchdown.

Pete hugged Stud like the play had won Trinity the state championship. Stud hugged him back and chuckled, not because anything was funny, but because the play might've been one of the most improbable things he had ever seen since he'd been around the game. "I think Bobby's dead," he said. "Brian too."

It was too bad for Bobby. He didn't get to see the

gorgeous ball he threw to Brian Bell. He also missed Brian giving maximum effort to haul in the pass. Bobby had a valid reason for missing the play; he was on his back, trying to breathe. But it was okay. There was always the film. Bobby could bask in the glory of the play during the next film session with Pete in the quarterbacks' room.

When he did get to his feet, Bobby was mobbed by teammates. It was okay that his breathing was still not under his control; the state of pure euphoria that surrounded him was enough to make him feel alive.

9

MEL WAITED OUT ON THE FIELD FOR BOBBY TO take a shower and get treatment. He caught the final play of the scrimmage—heading straight over from the airport to Trinity just in time—and was proud of his son. The touchdown pass to Brian Bell was all Mel needed to see. He was a believer, after all those years of disappointment.

Bobby exited the locker room and walked over with ice wraps on both shoulders. His ribs were raw to the touch and he had jammed his left ankle to boot.

"Hi son," Mel said.

"Hey Dad."

"That was some throw," Mel said. "You stood in there and got walloped."

Bobby winced as he readjusted the ice pack on his right shoulder, the more tender of the two.

"I won't make it to the first game of the season if this is how it's gonna be in practice," Bobby said.

"Yeah. I talked to Stud about it and he agreed. The defense is gonna ease up in practice a little bit. I told Stud that he shouldn't even let you guys hit each other in practice. Save it for the other team."

"You talked to Stud?"

"Yeah. Is that a problem?"

"I don't know. He's the coach. And you never talked to Stud before," Bobby said. "At least, not about football stuff. I can't even remember the last time I've seen you out at practice."

"Well, Bobby, that's because you've never been on the field."

"Please. Just don't get involved."

"Excuse me?"

"I can handle it," Bobby said. "I don't need you getting involved with Stud or anything else."

Mel stood up straight and faced his son.

"You need to watch your tone," he said. "Just because you're the starting quarterback doesn't mean that you can get away with mouthing off. And besides, I'm here to help you."

"I just don't want you involved," Bobby said. "You've never been there, you've never had the time. Now that I'm on the field, it just doesn't . . . "

Bobby took a deep breath and a needle of pain entered and exited the cartilage in between his ribs.

"It just doesn't feel right," Bobby said.

They were both silent now.

"I have to go back in for more treatment," Bobby said. "I'll see you at home."

Bobby turned around and slowly made his way back to the locker room.

Mel turned around and faced the field. It was his turn to take a deep breath. He'd had bad business deals over the years; even lost every cent to his name a couple of times. None of that hurt as much as this.

. . . .

Bobby drove himself home after getting the extra treatment on his shoulders and ankle. He drove slowly because he couldn't do anything fast at that moment. He also liked looking out of his window as he cruised home. The streets were lined with homes, and on the lawns of those homes were banners and flags that celebrated Trinity High School and its beloved football team. To say that football was a religion in Texas would not be an overstatement, embellishment, or lie. People lived and died with the results of their team, and Trinity's faithful were no different.

He slowed his car at the end of a block that was extraordinarily ornate. One house had a huge banner on its front lawn that read, "Go Trinity! See y'all at Jerry's World in November!" The message was a reference to the Texas Six-A Division One championship game held at Cowboys Stadium, which the locals called "Jerry's World." Bobby and his teammates were a long way from raising any banners of their own. The banner also displayed the jersey numbers of the Trinity players who were expected to contribute to the planned, but not yet achieved, championship season. These were the players that for the most part, had pedigrees in Texas football. They were known and revered for their repeated efforts on the field in the fall.

Bobby's number fifteen was not highlighted on the banner. As he drove a little farther down the block, though, he noticed another banner, set farther back on a lawn, closer to the house. This banner was just as big as the first one and read "We believe in you Bobby Dupree! #15." The vote of confidence didn't heap any more pressure onto Bobby's battered shoulders. There was no room left on them anymore. Stud's words about the season resting on his performance left more of an impression than anything else.

Before Bobby took a left turn on the road that led to his house, he took a detour to drive past Larissa Mumphrey's house. He stopped across the street, put his car in park, and looked out. There were no banners on Larissa's lawn. Her house was just about the only one on this street that did not make reference to Trinity High School's varsity football team.

What no one else in the world knew was that Bobby stopped across from Larissa's house on the way home from school every once in a while. He had done it ever since he had gotten his driver's license two years before. He was never weird or creepy about it. He never stayed for too long nor did he ever leer at her as she was coming or going. Just a few minutes here and there. Bobby would imagine what it would be like to walk up to the front door, knock, and pick up Larissa for a date. He then wondered what it would be like to walk Larissa to her door to give her a kiss after the date was over. Bobby would ponder those things and then drive home.

When Bobby was done daydreaming on that day, he rubbed his right shoulder and put his car in drive. Though Larissa had told him that she didn't date football players, he felt like he had a chance. The confidence from being on the field, from being "the man," emanated from Bobby now. Suddenly, there were possibilities due to the fact that he was finally in the game.

10

ON THE FRIDAY MORNING OF THE FIRST GAME OF the regular season, Bobby sat in his first period English class feeling relaxed. He felt prepared for his first ever start as quarterback. His classmates watched him closely, in an effort to ascertain if there were nerves or jitters. He stared back at them coolly. The girls, meanwhile, looked at him with adolescent lust in their eyes. He was a prize to be had now. Bobby didn't care about those girls though. The girl he liked, the one he wanted to get to know, was not interested in football and more importantly, she was not interested in football players. Winning

Larissa over would represent Bobby's biggest win of the season. So as his English teacher, Ms. Halston, stood in front of the class, chalk blotches on her black dress, hair tied up in a solemn bun, droning on and on about medieval poetry, Bobby sat calmly. He thought about the ways he could sway Larissa Mumphrey.

. . . .

Larissa was at her locker, grabbing a few of the books she needed for her classes after lunch. The entire school was infected with its annual first game fever. The girls wore the jerseys of their favorite players. The players walked around the halls like they owned them, chests out, eyes propositioning. Even the teachers and administrators were caught up in the hysteria. The administrators, in particular, knew how the school's bread was buttered.

But Larissa couldn't have cared less. Though

she had friends who were influenced by the state of football affairs, she wasn't the type to fall victim to the peer pressure game. She didn't go to games and rarely went to the after-parties anymore. She hadn't attended a single after-party, in fact, since freshman year.

Bobby spotted her from the end of the hall and hurried to catch up. She closed her locker and he quickened his pace.

"Larissa!" he called out, before finally reaching her. She turned and smiled.

"Shouldn't you be getting ready for tonight's game with the other Neanderthals?"

"Huh?"

"Football players never go to class on Fridays," she said. "They're too busy."

"For someone who doesn't like football, you seem to know a lot about it. Football players too."

"Well I know enough to know to stay away."

"You should also know that I do go to class," Bobby said. "See?"

He unzipped his book bag and revealed its contents to Larissa: binders, books, and pencils.

"That's very impressive," she said, with a twist of sarcasm. "I gotta meet up with some friends in the senior lounge."

She began to turn away and Bobby grabbed her by the arm. There was no aggression in the act, though it was firm.

Larissa turned to face Bobby, stunned by his forwardness. Bobby was stunned too. He had never done anything like that.

"I'm insulted that you think you have me figured out, without really taking the time to get to know me," he said. He let go of her arm.

"You mean you're not like other football players?" she asked, with sincerity in her eyes.

"I don't know what you mean," Bobby said. "Well, I guess I do. You're asking me if I go to class and not take them seriously? Or if I go to parties and hook up with a bunch of girls? And if I throw my weight around just because I play a game?"

Larissa stood there silent. He had impressed her by his ability to express his thoughts.

"Well the answers to those questions are, no, I go to class and pay attention. No, I don't go to parties. I've only been to a few. And no, I don't throw my weight around. Tonight will be my first time ever stepping on the field."

"You will," Larissa said, snapping out of the dream world where she would even give Bobby a chance to get close. "Once you get out on that field, you'll be just like the rest of them. The attention will go to your head, and you'll go to the place I'm talking about."

"I'm not like everyone else."

"Not yet," Larissa said.

"Come to the game tonight."

"What did I tell you the other day?"

"Come on, Larissa," Bobby pleaded. "Don't judge me. I'm not like the other guys on the team."

"We'll see," she said, before turning her back and walking down the hall.

When Larissa was out of sight, Bobby said, "You'll see."

* *

It was an hour before kickoff as Bobby stood on the field, looking into the stands and trying to put the thoughts of Larissa out of his mind. The stands were filling in and by kickoff, would be at full capacity. Bobby glanced up to where his parents and younger sister were sitting. His mom and sister waved to him at every chance, while his father was stoic in posture.

The players across the field from Trinity were from Plano High, a team in Trinity's section. Bobby stared at Plano's starting defense, and the first thing that jumped out was the unit's collective size. During that week's film study with Pete, he had seen that Plano's defense was big and aggressive. But seeing a team on film is one thing and witnessing it in person is another. Plano's defensive coaches knew that Bobby was stepping onto the field for the first time in his career. Plano would want to hit him early and often to find out if the career backup had any grit. Bobby knew he would have to protect himself during the game.

Overhead, the lights illuminating the field buzzed as they came to life. There was no Texas football without the lights. There was no better night than Friday. The stands were filled now. Bobby did a quick pre-game stretch and ran back into the locker room amid the shouts of encouragement from Trinity's fans. Bobby ignored the blind praise as well as the pageantry. None of it mattered to him. All of his thoughts and energy would go into the *game*.

The game.

That's all there was now. Even his thoughts of Larissa would have to wait until after he stepped off the field.

Larissa stood at the edge of the gate that allowed entrance to Pennington field, the site of Trinity's home games. She was about to do something that she promised herself she'd never do again. When she was a freshman at Trinity, she fell for a senior football player named Tommy Cignetti. At first things were fine—more than fine really. Tommy was one of the most popular players on the team and made Larissa feel like he really cared about her. They also had fun together, going to all the parties after Tommy's games. But one party at the end of freshman year changed her life. After getting too drunk and losing track of Tommy at some huge house in the suburbs, Larissa went searching through the rooms in an effort to find her boyfriend. She found Tommy in the home's master bedroom with her best friend Tammy. Seeing those two naked together shook her beer-soaked brain out of its haze. Though crushed, Larissa vowed to never go to another football party and she had kept that promise to herself. She also promised herself that she would never be with a football player ever again. All of this swirled inside her head as she waited at the gate, her indecisiveness fueled by fear and pain.

But regardless of the past, she was there, standing at the threshold of the gate. Her wounds had healed to the point of being intrigued by Bobby Dupree. She allowed the thought that maybe he *was* different. But she couldn't let him know that. Not yet, at least. The only way would be to watch Bobby from afar at first.

"You comin', 'Rissa?" her current best friend, Casey asked. "The quarterback of the team invited you to the game and you're sittin' there thinking it over. Let's go in!"

Casey Huffines was one of the girls who wore a Trinity jersey in the halls on game day. Other than the fact that they grew up together, the two friends were very different. Sometimes, Larissa wondered why they were even friends in the first place, but deep down she knew the answer to that question. Casey had shown herself to be a true friend when the stuff with Tommy happened during freshman year. That would always mean a lot to Larissa.

"I know you like him," Casey said. "You wouldn't be here if you didn't."

Larissa did not want to draw any attention to the fact that yes, maybe she did like Bobby Dupree. Casey was adept at picking up on the slightest movement of an eyebrow or curl of the lip, and then snuffing it all out from there. Then there'd be no end to it. Trinity's halls would be filled with rumor upon rumor about Larissa and Bobby. That was the last thing Larissa wanted.

"You talk too much," Larissa said finally.

A feeling in her gut said that she owed it to herself to find out if what Bobby said about himself was true. If he was, in fact, different. Larissa nodded toward the opening in the gate that led to the field, and Casey in turn, squealed in ecstasy. The two best friends walked through the gate, hand and hand, and through the swell of Trinity's fans.

11

BOBBY FELT GOOD PHYSICALLY AFTER A COUPLE of rough practices, but also knew that this would be the best his body would feel for a long time. He looked up to the sky right before Trinity received the opening kickoff. Not for religious reasons though. Really, he just liked looking at the Texas night sky. Under the usual circumstances, with Edmond healthy, Bobby would look up at the starless sky before kickoff, wearing a backwards cap and holding a clipboard. He'd tell himself to stay mentally engaged, though he knew deep down that he'd never see the field. Now, Bobby was wearing a helmet and ready to step onto the field.

Trinity opened the game at its own thirty-five yard line after a good kickoff return. Bobby trotted out to his first real huddle and knelt down inside the circle. He barked out the first play over the chants of both schools' fans. The stadium was loud—twelve thousand five hundred people—and, as was custom at Trinity, its fans stood until the offense converted a first down.

Bobby got up to the line and looked over Plano's defense. The nose tackle was three hundred pounds and their two defensive ends were each at least six foot five. Bobby lifted his right leg and stamped it back down into the ground. Brian Bell came into motion from right to left. Plano's defense shifted its alignment with him.

"Blue thirty-eight! Blue thirty-eight!"

Bobby couldn't hear anything on the field but the silence. A wondrous smile came onto his face as he focused on the twitchy hands of Plano's defensive linemen.

They want to tear my head off, he thought, before the smile morphed in an inexplicable cackle. "Go!"

On the snap, Bobby pitched the ball to Tevin going left. Trinity's offensive line sealed the edge and opened up an alley for Tevin to take the ball thirty yards, to Plano's thirty-five yard line.

Bobby looked over to Pete on the sideline for the next play. Once received, he re-entered the huddle and relayed the play call to the rest of the offense. The unit broke and made its way to the line of scrimmage. Bobby eyed Plano's free safety as the defender crept toward the line and into the box. The extra defender made it a loaded box. The play call was for another handoff to Tevin, a dive between the left guard and center. But Plano's free safety was there to fill that exact gap. Eight men in the box. Bobby knew what he had to do.

He stepped out from under center and hand-signaled Trinity's audible for a run-pass change to both receivers. He then called out "Slide Louie! Slide Louie!" to his offensive linemen. This alerted the line as to what the pass protection scheme was. When he was satisfied that everyone was on the same page with the audible, Bobby crouched back under the center and yelled, "Go!"

The ball was snapped and the free safety pushed toward the line of scrimmage. The offensive line slid to the left to pick up the extra pressure, and both the fullback and tailback helped out with pass protection on either edge. The pocket was clean. Bobby looked to the right and saw Brian Bell in one-on-one coverage. He threw the ball with the intention of placing it at the front-right pylon of the end zone. Brian, who had stepped on the cornerback, ran as fast as he could to the front pylon. He put his hands out, and the ball dropped into them for the touchdown.

Seven to nothing, Trinity over Plano.

After accepting head slaps from his offensive linemen, Bobby ran over to the sidelines. Trinity's fans, though simply ecstatic over the touchdown, also made sure to acknowledge Bobby for leading his first scoring drive as a starter. Edmond Daniels faded further away from the collective consciousness. Bobby was the one in their eyes now.

"Loaded box, Dupree!" Pete screamed at Bobby. He had both hands on Bobby's helmet. "Loaded box!"

Brian Bell came over and handed Bobby the touchdown ball.

"Oh no. You keep it," Bobby said, knowing it was Brian's habit to keep all of his touchdown balls.

"It's your first one," Brian replied. "Keep this one. 'Cause I'm gonna keep all the rest of them."

Bobby accepted it.

Then there was Stud. He was careful not to exude too much excitement. Stud knew how fickle the game was. He knew better than to get swept up in the emotion of *one* moment. He walked over to Bobby and looked him in the eyes.

"Nice play, Dupree."

He also gave Bobby a pat on the helmet before walking away.

In the stands, the Dupree family basked in the crowd's adoration for Bobby. Mel knew success in the business world, but was never good enough to make it on the field. Bobby was now a trailblazer in his own family.

Finally, there was Larissa Mumphrey's reaction. She didn't have much of one to the touchdown pass or the chaos around her in the stands. She covered her ears because the exuberance was at a deafening level. Larissa studied Bobby on the sidelines instead. She watched him to make sure he wouldn't become what she predicted, and to make sure he kept his promise.

Trinity's fight song repeated itself as the break in action after the kickoff allowed for that natural momentum boost for the scoring team. Bobby stood next to Pete on the sideline as Plano took possession of the ball for the first time.

"Now they know you can sting them," Pete said,

with a fatty in his lower lip. "They ain't gonna load the box like *that* anymore. They're not gonna just show it to you. They'll disguise it."

"I never realized it was this loud before," Bobby said.

"That's cause you're in it now," Pete said.

Plano's offense took the field and it was time to find out if Trinity's defense—with its reputation for relentless aggression—was all it was cracked up to be. Plano boasted an experienced quarterback, a massive offensive line, and weapons at the skill positions. Add it all up and you had the makings of an explosive offense. Plano came out in an I-formation, looking to pound Trinity with the run. On the first play, Plano ran a toss-sweep to the right, pulling a three-hundred pound guard directly at Tyrone. Tyrone not only avoided getting pancaked by the pulling guard, he also made a chest-to-chest tackle on Plano's running back, a player fifty pounds heavier than him. The play went for a loss of three.

On second down, Plano tried a deep pass, throwing to Tyrone's side. Tyrone intercepted the pass at midfield and ran the ball back to Plano's twenty-yard line. Tyrone sprinted off the field and onto Trinity's sideline.

"I told 'em not to test me!"

Bobby slapped a high-five with Tyrone, and then made his way over to where Stud and Pete stood. Bobby looked at Pete and asked, "Wanna go power?"

Pete started to answer, but Stud intervened.

"No," Stud said. "Kings. Six-ninety-nine, fullback choice. Let the X clear it out on the dig, and BB should be open on the nine. Putting Brian in the slot will throw their defense off."

"Got it," Bobby said, with a nod. He jogged onto the field and the home crowd quieted enough for him to call out the play just below full throat.

Brian smiled when he heard the play call because he knew the motion from right to left, into the slot position, would be like stealing for him. Opposing teams weren't used to seeing Brian line up in the slot. The tactic was a new wrinkle that Stud and Pete had put into the offense during off-season in an effort to free Brian up from attracting constant double-teams.

When the offense reached the line of scrimmage, the rationale for Stud's aggressive play call became clear to Bobby. Plano's defense had lost something—their defenders seemed indecisive and weren't itching to get to Bobby like on the first drive. Bobby's opening salvo had put Plano on the defensive, reacting to Trinity instead of attacking. It was time to step on Plano's throat.

Brian went in motion from right to left and took his spot in the slot, off the line of scrimmage. Bobby called out his cadence with a timbre that reinforced his growing confidence.

"Go!"

Bobby dropped seven steps. The offensive line was in unison, allowing enough time for him to go through his entire progression without the slightest hint of pressure. With a clean pocket, Bobby liked what he saw on the left: the X had cleared it out, like Stud had predicted, and Brian was one-on-one with a linebacker up the seam. Brian created five yards of separation between himself and the over-matched defender. All Bobby had to do was make the throw.

Bobby laid the ball out right over the goal line and Brian made a diving two-handed catch in the end zone—one of the prettiest touchdown catches of Brian Bell's Trinity career.

The execution of the play was a thing of beauty. Bobby celebrated with his offensive lineman and then looked over to Pete, who shot his quarterback the gunman's salute. Brian Bell kept this ball like he said he would. Bobby's teammates mobbed him when he got over to the sideline. Stud gave him another tempered pat on the back of the helmet. Fourteen to nothing Trinity. Trinity's fight song droned on, long into the black Texas night, closing in on Plano with every refrain.

By the time the full damage had been done, Trinity had beaten Plano by a score of forty-one to ten. Bobby finished the game by completing fifteen of sixteen passes for two hundred fifty-three yards and four touchdowns passes. He did not throw any interceptions. Even Edmond Daniels had not started his Trinity career in this fashion. The most impressive aspect of Bobby's night was that he did the majority of his damage in the first half when the game's outcome was in question. Trinity was up thirty-five to zero at the intermission.

Stud pulled Bobby out of the game for good after one drive in the third quarter. This was done, partially out of respect for Plano as running up the score on an opponent was not looked upon kindly, but the main reason for Stud pulling Bobby out was fear of injury.

Bobby, for his part, was okay with coming out of

the game in the third and did not protest his head coach's decision. He was used to being on the sideline during blowouts, but those stories were always penned by someone else. As the clock ticked down and showed all zeroes, he didn't think of how far he had come in a short period of time. Bobby thought about Larissa Mumphrey instead.

Larissa left the game to go home during halftime. She declined Casey's invitation to the post-game party at some big house or another in the suburbs. Larissa studied Bobby throughout the entire first half, finding his demeanor levelheaded enough for further fact-finding. She was afraid to admit to herself that she liked what she saw in Bobby Dupree. He didn't behave like a cocky fool out there on the field—mighty impressive considering the success he had experienced that night. When Larissa got to her car in the parking lot adjacent to Pennington field, she'd decided she would give Bobby Dupree a chance. That is, if he came calling again.

After a post-game shower, Bobby exited the locker room with a couple of his offensive lineman. They stopped to speak with a group of girls wearing Trinity jerseys. As if the uniforms weren't enough to express their allegiance, each member of the group had a Trinity-colored heart painted on her face. Casey Huffines was with the group. Trinity's left tackle, Troy Degarmo, put a meaty forearm around Casey's waist.

"Nice game, Bobby Dupree," Casey said.

"Thanks."

"Larissa was up there in the stands with me," she said. "But she left at half-time."

"Larissa came?" Bobby said, his eyes lighting up.

"Yeah."

"Let's get out of here, Dupree," Degarmo said, losing interest in Bobby and Casey's exchange.

Bobby shook his head dubiously and rubbed at his right shoulder. "I don't know, Troy. I'm kind of—"

"You're not getting out of it that easy, Dupree," Degarmo said. "You *have* to come to this party."

"Is Larissa coming?" Bobby asked Casey.

She shook her head.

"Tonight you'll hang with the big boys," Degarmo butted in, putting his arm around Bobby's shoulder. "You're one of us now."

Bobby's posture revealed that he was less than enthusiastic about the invitation. Degarmo was undaunted however.

"On Monday you can fall in love with Larissa," Degarmo said.

12

THE PARTY WAS ALREADY IN FULL EFFECT BY THE time Bobby had arrived with Degarmo, Casey, and the rest of their group. Most of the team was present at the party and every group was represented: black, white, Hispanic. Football was the connective tissue. Bobby didn't see Brian or Tyrone, though, two of the biggest stars on the team.

"Want a beer?" Degarmo asked Bobby, while pulling a few bottles out of the refrigerator by their necks.

"You just go into the fridge?" Bobby replied, looking around the kitchen, where people were drinking, making out at various levels of intensity, and smoking marijuana. "Whose house is this?"

Degarmo shrugged his mountainous shoulders. "I don't know and I don't care. It's time to get drunk." The big left tackle spoke with assuredness.

Bobby shook his head.

"Well, you want one?" Degarmo asked, holding a bottle out to Bobby.

Bobby didn't really want the beer but knew his teammates were watching him. He *had* to fit in or else risk stunting his early momentum as quarterback.

"Sure," Bobby said.

He took a sip of the beer and the bitterness of it reminded him of the other few times he'd had beer, with his Dad at Cowboys games.

"There's a lot of ass here tonight, Dupree," Degarmo said, lording out over the crowd in the kitchen.

"You're with Casey," Bobby said. "What do you care?"

Degarmo leaned in close. "I'm not *with* her right now, man."

Bobby nodded his head.

"You could clean up," Degarmo added. "With how you played tonight? New starting quarterback on the block."

Degarmo whistled.

"You could have a different girl every weekend."

And with that, Casey, materialized next to Degarmo, as if appearing out of thin air. She looked glassy-eyed, which seemed a bit odd to Bobby because they hadn't been at the party that long. She pulled on Degarmo's arm and led him toward an ascending stairwell leading out of the kitchen. Degarmo looked back to Bobby and smiled as he followed Casey upstairs.

Bobby leaned back against the counter next to the refrigerator.

"Hey there, Dupree," a female voice said from the side.

He looked over and saw Dana Killigan. Dana was known for sleeping with many of Trinity's football players. Bobby knew of her. Every male student at Trinity did.

"Dana," Bobby said, "right?"

Dana nodded and Bobby could tell just by the way she moved her head, that she was drunk. She reached down and put her hand on his thigh.

"I don't know where you came from," Dana said, her eyes almost looking past Bobby as she spoke. "But you are sure cute."

"I've always been here," Bobby said. "We had history together in seventh grade—"

She smiled and closed her eyes. Dana seemed like she was going to fall asleep right on Bobby's shoulder.

"You okay?" Bobby asked.

"Huh?" Dana said. "Yeah. I want to take you upstairs."

"Upstairs?" Bobby said. "What's upstairs."

She reached down and touched his thigh, this time closer to his crotch. "That's what's upstairs," she said.

"You don't even know me."

"I know you, Bobby Dupree," her words were slurring now.

Bobby was a virgin, having never even come close to this moment before.

"I don't know," Bobby said. "You're pretty drunk. I don't want you to do anything you might regret or—"

"Oh come on," Dana said, closing her eyes again. After she opened them up, she leaned in and gave Bobby a wet kiss. He enjoyed her tongue rolling around his mouth. In that moment, Bobby understood, for the first time really, the appeal of having female company. Dana moaned softly as she pulled away from Bobby. She bit her lower lip.

Bobby thought about Larissa just then. Perhaps it made sense to get *it* out of the way with Dana first. Bobby had heard things from teammates. He had heard that everyone's first time is sloppy. Bobby wanted to be experienced for Larissa. Maybe Dana would be the experience he needed.

"Okay," Bobby said.

Dana led him upstairs where there were rooms on both sides of a long hallway. Each door was closed until they reached an open one at the end. The music from the party below thumped with a persistence that made it hard to think.

"Here we are," Dana said dreamily.

Bobby walked into the dimly lit room first, and Dana closed the door behind them before plopping onto the bed, where she lay on her back and arched up her neck to eye him. Bobby looked around the room. Bed, dresser, matching bedside stands. It didn't look like a kid's room, and that detail comforted Bobby. It would've been weird having sex in a kid's room.

"Coming?" Dana asked.

"Yeah."

"Well hurry up already," she whined.

Bobby crept closer until getting onto the bed. He didn't know what to do next and hoped that Dana would lead the way. With her reputation, that shouldn't have been a problem. She elevated herself and met Bobby, so they were face to face, both on their knees. They kissed again, sloppily. Dana's breath sort of grossed Bobby out, reeking of old beer and cigarettes, but he didn't dare mention it. She snorted air out through her nose in between kisses, and at the next interval of reprieve, unbuttoned Bobby's shirt. He had no idea what came next. In the porn that he watched on his laptop in his room, the girls were already naked by the time the sex occurred. Dana still had clothes on.

The next moment Bobby found himself stripped down to his boxers. Dana pulled off her shirt and had no bra on underneath.

This is really happening, Bobby thought.

Dana peeled off her skin-tight jeans, the bottoms of which caught around her ankles before she ripped them off. Dana turned to Bobby and it was then, even in her blotto state, that Dana knew something was up.

Her eyes focused. A knowing, experienced smile appeared on her face.

"This is your first time, right?" she whispered.

"It's that obvious?" Bobby asked, looking past her.

"It's okay," she said. "We'll take it slow."

Dana seemed to relish the role of leader. That was fine by Bobby—exactly how he wanted it, in fact. She was experienced, and knew exactly what to do. She took it slow, and when they finished, Bobby could see why his teammates killed themselves to get it done on the field, if this was the reward.

"How was it?" Bobby asked shyly. "How was I?"

Dana smiled. "You were fine, Bobby Dupree. It'll get easier each time. Just like on the field. Tonight was your first game. But you'll get better. Think of it like that."

A sudden warmth came over Bobby and he wanted to be close to Dana. He got back onto the bed and leaned into her. Dana, though jarred, backed away politely.

"That was great," Bobby said.

"What?"

"Let's be together," Bobby said.

"*Be* together?"

"Yes," Bobby said. In the post-sex glow, Bobby had forgotten who Dana was. This wasn't about football or even love for her. He didn't know that Dana was a kind of vampire—she had to have Bobby Dupree. There was no choice to be made. For her, this was about something that Bobby couldn't wrap his mind around. And she was in no mood to explain it to him.

"I don't think so, Bobby," she said, touching his face. "Just the once."

Bobby sprung off the bed and put his clothes on with haste. He felt the urge to say something but knew he couldn't. Instead, he opened the door to the hallway and looked out. No one was out there, though some of the other doors were open too. He could hear a new song playing downstairs. Accompanied by acoustic guitar, a woman sang a haunting tune that filled the space around Bobby and Dana. Bobby looked back to Dana as she lay in the bed, satiated, and still topless. He listened again to the music, which was serious compared to the "fun" people were having at the party. He didn't say anything to Dana. He just stared at her.

Across the hall, Casey opened up the door to the room she and Degarmo had occupied and saw Bobby Dupree, with a horrified look on his face, standing in the doorway opposite her. Though drunk and high on Percocets, she was positive that was Bobby Dupree in that room. She retreated and closed the door, leaving it ajar. She peered through the crack, and Bobby had no idea he was being watched.

A stark thought entered Bobby's mind as he observed Dana silently: he hoped he hadn't screwed things up with Larissa and that this encounter wouldn't come back to haunt him. He shuddered, left the room, and then went downstairs, slipping out of the party unnoticed.

Casey, meanwhile, looked back into the room she was in and saw Degarmo fast asleep on the bed. He always fell asleep right after sex, and if that wasn't annoying enough, his bassy snoring drove her mad. She opened the door all the way and walked across the hall to the open room from which Bobby had just left. When she poked her head inside, she heard a light snoring. A girl's snoring. She looked at the bed to see Dana in her underwear, asleep, with no top on. Casey took a couple more steps and saw the shiny condom wrapper on the nightstand to the right of the bed.

Casey smiled as the woman singing over the acoustic guitar warned her lover that the next time would be the last time. Casey wasn't smiling because she planned on telling Larissa that Bobby had slept with Dana. She smiled because she had the proof she needed on Dana. Casey took solace in the fact she wasn't the only girl at Trinity High who slept with football players to feel better about herself.

13

A T SCHOOL, ON THE FOLLOWING MONDAY,
Bobby walked through Trinity's halls with a
feeling of self-loathing that he couldn't shake. He
didn't relish in the milestone of losing his virginity
that weekend. He was convinced that Larissa would
find out somehow, and when she did, he'd be dead
in her eyes. Beyond the feelings of paranoia, Bobby
felt that he had betrayed Larissa, even though they
weren't together. He tried to remind himself that
the unreasonable feelings were in sharp contrast to
the facts: no one had been upstairs to see Bobby
with Dana, and Dana herself was the only true

danger to Larissa and him. Dana's reaction to the sex reassured him that, to her, it was unattached. But he couldn't be sure that she would never tell.

Bobby could feel the eyes of his fellow students as he passed them in the halls that day. Dana locked eyes with him briefly in front of her locker before continuing on her way. There was no malevolence in her eyes, so Bobby walked on.

Casey bumped into Bobby in the halls too. She hadn't decided what to do with her powerful secret. Larissa was her best friend, but she wasn't convinced that telling her the truth was the best thing to do. Casey could tell that Larissa really liked Bobby, and the revelation would ruin their chances of being together. Casey also sympathized with Bobby; she too had made some poor choices with regard to who she slept with, but that didn't mean she was a bad person.

She watched Bobby as he made his way to first period. The underclassmen girls flitted around him like hummingbirds, while the upperclassmen ones put more into it with less effort—their bodies more developed, their lips fuller, and more equipped to tempt the new hot-shot quarterback.

Bobby didn't bite on any one of the overtures, and because of that Casey thought maybe she shouldn't tell Larissa. Maybe she should allow Bobby and Larissa to have a chance as a couple? That's really all Casey wanted for herself. She didn't want to be with a guy like Degarmo. She wanted someone who would treat her well and enjoy being with her.

Casey walked to her first period history class and took her seat next to Larissa in the front.

"Hey," Larissa said, opening her binder and taking out a pen.

"Hi," Casey said. "Where were you all weekend?"

"I went camping with my cousins at Eisenhower State Park."

"Oh."

"Well?"

"Well *what?*" Casey asked.

"What happened Friday night? Did you do it again?"

"Do what?"

Larissa leaned in close. "Troy?" she whispered.

"Yes."

Larissa shook her head. This was where the two best friends differed most from one another: when Larissa Mumphrey had an opinion about something, she shared it.

"How could you sleep with that gorilla again?" Larissa asked, still at a whisper. "He doesn't care about you. Next week, there'll be another football party. And he'll be with another girl. He's not gonna change unless you put your foot down and tell him 'no.'"

Casey held her words as tight as she could.

"I mean, come on, Casey," Larissa said. "Have a little self-respect."

This comment stung, and Casey couldn't help it anymore.

"What, like Bobby Dupree?"

"What about him?' Larissa asked, leaning in now.

"He was at the party Saturday night," Casey said, lowering her voice.

Larissa was quiet. She didn't want to hear what would come next, because she knew what it would be. Larissa had wanted to give Bobby Dupree a chance.

"I saw him leave a room where Dana was lying in bed, naked," Casey said, placing the blade in Larissa's gut. "So spare me your lecture."

Casey leaned back and a wave of sickness filled her stomach. Just five minutes before walking into the classroom, she had planned on keeping the secret to herself. But Larissa had pushed her, and Casey was incapable of holding her tongue when pushed. That sick feeling quickly changed into sadness because she knew that her friendship with Larissa was over.

Larissa sat there, frozen in her chair. She seemed to stay in that pose until the bell shook her back into reality fifty-five minutes later.

· ·

Bobby drummed up the courage to seek out Larissa during lunch. The event with Dana was an eyeopener; the feeling of being tossed aside after sex was still fresh in his mind. But beyond the hurt, the experience was a good thing. Now that Bobby had tasted sex, he knew what to expect and also realized he didn't want a girl like Dana who liked him just because he was on the football team or for some other reason altogether. He knew he wanted someone like Larissa, someone who cared.

When he walked into the cafeteria, he spotted Casey across the way, but no Larissa. Bobby approached and sat next to Casey at a cafeteria table.

"Hi Casey," Bobby said. "Have you seen Larissa around?"

Casey looked down.

"Everything okay?"

She raised her head and averted Bobby's eyes. If he'd had more experience at this, he'd have been able to read this sign. But he had no clue about girls.

Casey shook her head. "I saw her during first period," she said. "I don't know where she is now."

"She left school?"

"I don't know, Bobby. Check the parking lot. She's probably in her car," she said. "I have to go."

Casey stood up from the cafeteria table and left in a hurry. That, Bobby did notice. *Something is up,* he thought.

Bobby made his way out to the student parking lot and began to look for Larissa's black Honda Civic. He knew her car from the secret trips to her house. After a few minutes, he spotted the compact car, and walked over to it slowly, his caution stemming from the movement in the driver's side. When Bobby got close enough to realize that it was indeed Larissa's car and that she was the person moving around in the driver's seat, he took a deep breath and leaned down into the open passenger's side window. Larissa's head was turned the other way.

Nirvana's "Come as You Are" emanated from one of the speakers.

"Hi Larissa," Bobby said. "I've been looking for you."

She turned her head slowly and faced Bobby. It was clear that she had been crying.

"What's wrong?"

"I heard about the party, Bobby," Larissa said. "You *made* me like you, and then you made me look like a total idiot. Get away from me."

"Heard what?" Bobby asked, pathetically. "I didn't go to the party after the game. I went home."

Larissa got out of the car and slammed the door. She walked around to where Bobby stood.

"Now you are going to lie to me? I know you were there. Casey told me."

Bobby stayed quiet. He was rattled more so than from any hit he had taken on the field in the last couple of weeks. He wished he hadn't lied—he instantly knew that it was going to make this worse.

"And that's not all she told me. She said you had sex with Dana."

Bobby panicked, sweat formed on his forehead and he shook his head, as if to make himself believe that he really hadn't slept with Dana.

"That . . . "

"That what?" Larissa said, right in his face.

He didn't know what to say. He just stood still.

"I told you," she said, a fat tear dribbling down her cheek. "You're just like the rest of them."

"I'm not," Bobby said. "I'm different."

Larissa shook her head. "No, you're not. I was even fooled for a second. And I really hoped that what you told me was true. But you're not who you think you are."

Bobby still couldn't speak. All he could do was stare at Larissa. He couldn't help but fixate on the hurt in her eyes. He never knew that he could hurt someone like this. He never thought that he could matter this much.

"Larissa," he said.

"Just get away from me," she said, with a deep breath. "Leave me alone."

"Larissa, I can explain."

She turned her back to him, got back into her car and turned the music up louder.

Bobby stood there for another minute or two, trying to understand what had happened before walking back into school. Even though Bobby and Larissa weren't boyfriend and girlfriend, even though they had never even kissed, he knew that he had let something special slip away.

14

THE STANDS AT THAT DAY'S PRACTICE WERE MORE densely populated due to the team's success in the first game. Many of the new people out at practice were wearing cowboy hats. These old men were both Dallas businessmen and Trinity alums who couldn't wait to get another peek at Bobby Dupree. They were thrilled at the fact that Trinity's new hope was a good-looking white kid from an established family. After seeing Mel's boy light the Plano High defense up in person, they began dangling the promise of donations in exchange for access to the practice field. Stud wasn't thrilled with this arrangement. He liked to keep his practice field as close-knit as possible. But the prospects of financial gain for the school and athletic department were too important to those higher on the food chain.

Mel Dupree on the other hand, made sure not to stand with the men wearing the cowboy hats, going so far as leaving his Stetson at home. Although Mel was interested in Bobby's play, he respected his son's wishes and watched from afar. It broke his heart to stay away at first, but after a few lonely nights with the bottle, he decided that Bobby was right. When things got tough for his son—and they would—Bobby would have to go through it on his own.

Bobby noticed the added presence at practice—and the way Mel stood apart from it—but was in no mood for anything extra to consume his thoughts. In fact, his mind was elsewhere altogether. He didn't know how to patch things up with Larissa. He didn't even know where to begin. The major problem now was that Bobby wanted to be with Larissa more than ever.

His warmup throws were not crisp, his mind simply too cluttered. The truth was he didn't even feel like being out there. A passing wish to go back to second string crossed through his mind.

Pete and Stud stood at a distance from Bobby. They knew something was up. Many coaches at the high school level spent more time with their players than the players spent with their families.

"I was afraid of this," Stud said.

"You think the pressure is getting to him already?" Pete asked. "After one game?"

"Could be that," Stud said. "Or it could be thirty-two different things. He's a teenage boy. What did we say to Edmond all time? Consistency. Well, it took Edmond a good half-season to show consistency. And that's with the talent Edmond had."

Stud blew his whistle, signifying the start of practice.

It was clear after the first drill, that Stud's fear about lack of consistency in Bobby's play was real.

Pete came over to Bobby after one particularly

poor throw, to remind him about his mechanics. Bobby nodded an affirmation but could not focus enough to grasp Pete's suggestion. Bobby then made the same mistake during the next rep, and then a new one on the following one, all of which made Pete and Stud scratch their heads even more. Up to that point, Bobby's best attribute was that he did not let failure on one play snowball into something bigger. His sudden lack of attention was disturbing.

During one-on-ones, after a terrible overthrow on a nine route, Stud pulled Bobby out and put Mickey in for a few reps. Bobby went over to get a drink of water and dropped to one knee. He couldn't stop thinking about Larissa and how much he had hurt her. The worst part of it was that his chance with Larissa had ended before it had really started.

Then, there was Mel. He was just standing there, staring at his son. Bobby could feel his eyes burning a hole in his helmet.

Pete walked over and patted Bobby on the back of the shoulder pads.

"What's up?"

"Hey Coach," Bobby said, standing up to meet Pete's eyes.

"What's going on with you?" Pete asked. "You look a little—"

"I'm okay," Bobby said quickly, thinking that this is what he *should* be saying. "I'll be fine."

"If you're feeling a little bit of pressure, or if you want to talk to somebody, I want you to know that you can talk to me or Stud."

Bobby took another squirt of water and pulled his helmet on.

"Okay?"

"Okay," Bobby said.

. . . .

"Can I see you in my office, Bobby?" Stud said, in the locker room, as Bobby was changing.

"Yeah, Coach."

He followed Stud into his office and sat down

in front of him. Bobby looked up at the wall over Stud's desk where all of the memorabilia from over the seasons hung: game balls from legendary contests, clippings from local newspapers, a jersey worn by Stud himself when he was the starting quarterback at Trinity.

"Is everything alright with you?" Stud asked. "We were hoping that because you played so well on Friday night, we'd be able to build on it this week."

"I think I just had an off day," Bobby said, once again saying something that he thought Stud would like to hear.

"I understand if you're feeling pressure," Stud said. "I've been in that same chair that you're sitting in right now."

Bobby didn't reply. It wasn't the football part that was troubling him. He didn't feel any pressure to perform on the field. Yet. And besides, from where he came from on the depth chart, just *being* on the field was enough. If he played well, it'd be a bonus.

"What is it? Your dad?"

"No, Coach," Bobby said. "My dad has actually been okay. He's watching, but from a distance, like I asked him to."

"Then what is it?"

Bobby thought that maybe it would help to tell Stud about Larissa, but quickly threw cold water on the notion. It was too embarrassing.

"I'm going to be fine, Coach," Bobby said. "I'm getting used to all the reps. Sometimes my arm feels a little tired."

He pinned it on his arm because it was easier that way. Bobby's arm was fine.

Stud stood up from his desk.

"Something is up with you. I'm here to help you. You can tell me—whatever it is."

Bobby remained silent.

Stud kept talking, his voice rising as he spoke, "I'm not gonna let this season go down the tubes because you're too stubborn to let us help you. We've got a championship defense. And what I need from you is to go out there and play like you did on Friday night. Son, you are not gonna get better unless it happens on the practice field first. So if something is wrong in class. Or at home. Or with one of your teammates, I need you to tell me so I can fix it for you."

Bobby stared at his coach.

Stud sighed and softened his tone a bit, "Do you understand?"

"Yes," Bobby replied. "Nothing is bothering me, Coach."

15

OVER THE NEXT THREE WEEKS, TRINITY WON ALL three of its games by a combined score of one hundred and ten to fifty-five. The 4-0 record was good enough for a share of first place in their section after a month of play. Bobby played well in the three games, compiling an average of two hundred and fifty yards per game with seven touchdowns and one interception. He also added a running score. Still, he was not playing with the looseness he had displayed early on, and it was due to his sadness over Larissa.

Trinity's next game would be an undefeated

showdown with its rival, Katy High School, from nearby Katy, Texas. This was an important game for Trinity. This was the game that Trinity had lost in bitter fashion the year before when Edmond Daniels threw a pick-six to end a potential game-winning drive. That game was at Katy High. This one would be at Pennington field.

Bobby saw Larissa in passing on numerous occasions in the halls. He tried to make eye contact a few times, but she wasn't having it. In the week after the argument, Bobby once again stopped in front of her house a few times, but didn't have the heart to get out of the car and knock on the door. After a couple of weeks passed, Bobby stopped passing by her house and chose a different route to get to his.

The cowboy hats were out in full effect during the week of practice prior to the Katy game. Bobby couldn't believe how many hands he had to shake before and after practice that week. Most of the handshakes were with the men who wore the cowboy hats. These men urged Bobby to win, and a few even intimated that a loss to Katy was out of the question, an impossibility, and finally, downright unacceptable. They insinuated that the ramifications from a loss in the Katy game would be disastrous for Stud, Bobby, and the rest of Trinity's team. Bobby took it all in stride the best way he knew how. He got into the Katy game-plan and learned it inside and out.

One night, he even spent a few minutes running through the playbook with his father. He noticed that Mel hadn't been drinking quite as much, and was listening more than he was talking. For the first time in a while, Mel Dupree was somebody Bobby could count on to keep him calm and focused.

· ·

The Friday of the Katy game was always an off day for the students of Trinity High. It was the job of Trinity's faithful to use the random day off as a means of resting up and making sure Pennington

Field was as loud as could be for the big game. Education could wait when it came to beating Katy. That went for everybody at Trinity. Even teachers and administrators were expected to participate in the effort. With Friday classes off, it was another Trinity tradition for the starters to go out to dinner together on the Thursday night before the Katy game. Each season, twenty-two Trinity players would shower up after Thursday's practice, go out to one burger joint or another, and finally, end the night with some mild shenanigans.

Bobby wasn't excited about this tradition, having never been invited to take part before. But what choice did he have now? He was the starting quarterback, and there was just no way his teammates would let him skip the occasion.

Sure enough, later that night Bobby found himself sitting at a four-top in an old fashioned drive-in that boasted the best burgers in North Texas. He munched on his burger and sipped his Coke in silence, while most of his fellow teammates yapped about what they would do in the Katy game, and to the girls of Trinity after. When Bobby was finished with his meal, the owner of the drive-in came over along with a young boy.

"Bobby," the owner said. "My son and I were hoping we could get a picture with you."

Bobby chuckled. "Sure."

"My boy wants to play quarterback at Trinity, just like you," the owner said. "He starts for his pee-wee team now."

Bobby stood up and the owner's son approached. He put his arm around the boy's shoulder and a waitress snapped a few pictures of them.

"You go get Katy," the owner demanded. "Get 'em good."

"Yes, sir," Bobby said. "Good luck to you and your son."

The rest of the starters were finished eating and milling around the entrance to the drive-in. They were pretty much broken up into position groups, with a few exceptions. Bobby stood next to the offensive lineman because it felt natural to do so.

"I'm ready to get wasted! Right now!" Degarmo said, definitively. "Where are we going?"

"There's a Trinity party over in Euless," someone said.

"Is it cool if we all roll?" someone else posed.

Bobby paced in small arcs, hands stuffed into the pockets of his hoodie. He was hoping that it wouldn't be okay for everyone to show up to this party in Euless. He really wanted to go home and get in bed.

"Yeah, we can all roll," someone called out.

There was a collective rush of energy when the destination of the party was set. A rush that Bobby was not a part of. He tried slipping away to his car, but that attempt was squashed by Degarmo, as always, loudly.

"Where you going, Dupree?"

"I'm gonna go home," Bobby said. "I need some rest."

"Home?" Degarmo boomed, his tone bringing everyone into the conversation. "Uh-uh. You're coming out. We step out on that field together. We stick together."

Bobby felt crowded. He couldn't know what each one of his teammates was thinking, but it was clear to him that their mindset was something similar to Degarmo's. It was hard to tell. But with a quick scan of his teammates' eyes, he thought that maybe he did have a choice. And perhaps some of his teammates felt the same pressure to attend the party that he did. Neither they nor Bobby spoke up about those desires, however.

"Okay," Bobby said, nodding his head. He stuffed his hands back into his hoodie and followed the crowd to the caravan of cars that would make its way to the party in Euless.

When players arrived at the party, it was spilling out onto the front lawn of a sprawling suburban home.

Bobby walked to the front door of the house with Degarmo and another offensive lineman.

"I need to find Casey 'cause I need some ass tonight!" Troy called out to no one in particular.

The inside of the party was similar to the first one of the season that Bobby had attended. A pretty, blonde-haired junior brushed by Bobby on two separate occasions and finally invited him upstairs. He turned her down as politely as one possibly could.

Degarmo looked down at Bobby, shaking his head.

"You are a hard-headed moron, Dupree," Degarmo said.

Bobby ignored the comment as they made their way through the house and outside to a deck overlooking the backyard, where more partygoers were extracting beer from a keg. Bobby spotted Casey down on the lawn before Degarmo did, and without bringing attention to himself, made his way down to her.

"Casey," Bobby said.

"Hi, Bobby," she said.

"Have you seen Larissa around?"

"We don't really talk anymore, after, you know," she said, looking past Bobby and up to Dagarmo. She rolled her eyes at his sight. "What's that asshole doing here?"

"Troy?" Bobby said. "I thought you two—"

"No," she said, abruptly.

She left Bobby and walked up the stairs. Degarmo saw her, and when she didn't stop to talk, he grabbed her arm. She ripped it away before going back into the house.

Bobby witnessed this from the lawn. Degarmo didn't look as cool as he claimed to be from down there. Degarmo looked down on the lawn and saw Bobby. He walked over to the edge of the deck and whistled.

"Dupree!"

Bobby walked close to the deck and looked up at his left tackle. He nodded.

"There any more beer in that thing?" Degarmo said, nodding to keg.

Bobby looked back at it and saw people filling up full cups of beer.

"I think so."

Degarmo nodded and he and a few other offensive linemen walked down the stairs and over to the keg. Bobby followed. Degarmo knew his way around a keg. He poured four beers for himself and his teammates, and made sure to note that none of the pours had much foam.

"What's going on with you and Casey?" Bobby asked.

"Everything comes to an end, Dupree," Degarmo replied, serving another beer to a thirsty hand around him. "Forget her."

He held a beer out to Bobby. Bobby stuffed his hands into his hoodie.

"I'm good, thanks," he said.

Degarmo and the other linemen left Bobby on the lawn and went back inside the house. After the keg was tapped, Bobby stood on the lawn alone. He turned away from the party and looked out into the blackness behind the house, focusing on the fact that all parties end, and that he would be able to go home soon. After a moment, there was a tap on his shoulder. Bobby turned and saw Brian Bell.

"What's up?"

"Hey, Brian," Bobby said, "Nothing much. Just looking at, well nothing."

They both chuckled.

"I normally don't like coming to these," Brian said. "But you know, the Katy game."

"Yeah, I know," Bobby said.

"Looks like you are one of the few guys not getting drunk," Brian said. "There's a few of us on the team. Me. Tyrone. Phil. You usually won't see us at these parties."

Brian was referring to Phil Boat, Trinity's starting strong-side linebacker.

"I noticed that," Bobby said. "I never know how

to handle this stuff. I feel like if I don't show up, I'll let the guys down or something."

"Well, me, Phil, and Tyrone, you know—we love the rest of the guys, but do our own thing," Brian said. "Tyrone's a church-goin' type, so it's easy for him to say no."

"And you?"

"Church?" Brian said. "Nah. But that don't mean that I mess with all these little freaks runnin' around these parties."

Brian chin-nodded a couple of girls, who were late to the party and dismayed at the void inside the keg.

"I just come to these things once in a while to keep the guys happy. I got me one girl. Been with her since freshman year. That's enough for me," Brian said. "No drama. Just football for me. Trying to get a scholarship, you know?"

"Yeah."

"You got a girlfriend?"

Bobby thought of Larissa. He shook the thought out of his head.

"No," he said.

. . . .

The party in Euless was beginning to die down a couple of hours later as Bobby and Brian made their way through the house and to the front yard. A few of their teammates stood out there too. The street was mostly quiet.

"I'm ready to get up out of here," Brian said.

"Me too," Bobby said.

Just then, the front door burst open and a blonde girl with her top torn open dashed onto the front lawn. Her bra was exposed and the black eyeliner she wore ran down her face. The fly of her tight, white jeans was open as well.

"Keep him away from me!" she screamed. "Keep him away!"

"Come back here!" Degarmo boomed, stomping out into the front yard.

The girl ran behind a car in the driveway. Degarmo tried to approach, but Bobby, Brian and two other large teammates restrained him.

"Ease up!" Brian said. "Chill out, Troy!"

"That stupid bitch bit me!" Degarmo said.

He stopped struggling when he realized that his teammates were in control. The girl's faint sobs filled the quiet, officially rendering the party dead. Everyone who remained inside was now outside, ready to leave, but fearful about what they might miss. Bobby saw rage in Degarmo's eyes; he didn't want to poke at Degarmo's aggression, so he stayed quiet. Instead, Bobby turned his attention to the blonde girl in distress. He walked over to her behind the car.

Bobby could see fear in her eyes.

"You okay?" he asked.

She replied with a shiver.

Bobby took off his hoodie and gave it to her. After she put it on, he leaned in close.

"What happened?"

Her teeth were rattling violently, and she was able to control her limbs enough to wipe the snot from her nose with the sleeve of Bobby's hoodie. "He wouldn't stop. I told him no, and he just wouldn't stop."

"Wait here. I'm gonna take you home." Bobby said.

Bobby walked over to Degarmo and the rest of his teammates. Some of them were laughing, while others, including Brian, waited for instruction on what to do next.

"What did you do?" Bobby demanded from Degarmo, in a tone that raised the eyebrows of everyone outside.

"Chill out," Degarmo said. "She bit me because she's nuts. She told me to go upstairs with her. Then she decides she doesn't want to do it."

"So, did you stop touching her?" Bobby asked.

"You are such a girl, Dupree," Degarmo answered.

Bobby lunged at Degarmo and grabbed him by the collar of his letterman jacket.

The rest of the guys broke Bobby and Troy apart.

"Look at little benchwarmer, Dupree," Degarmo said, with sober eyes. "What are you? The protector of all of Trinity's little whores?"

"You're done," Bobby said, pointing a finger right at Degarmo. "I'm getting out of here."

Bobby began to leave.

Degarmo's eyes widened. "Done? What do you mean? Come back here Dupree!"

"Hey, Bobby!" Brian called out. "Can I catch a ride?"

"Yeah," Bobby said.

Brian caught up with Bobby.

Bobby and Brian helped the blonde girl into Bobby's car. Degarmo stood there pouting, as he watched his two teammates assist the girl. Bobby had shown his heart in front of almost the entire team. There wasn't anything Degarmo could say or do to intimidate him.

Bobby got the girl's address before she fell asleep in the backseat. They got into the car, and Bobby pulled away from the house.

"I'm gonna tell Coach about this. First thing in the morning," Bobby said.

He looked over to Brian and for a while Brian didn't respond. He simply looked back at Bobby.

"I have a sister, man," Bobby said. "This isn't cool."

When they reached the girl's house, Bobby woke her up and helped her to the front door. He left his hoodie with her. She gave him a hug before she walked inside. Bobby got back into the car and the two headed toward Brian's house.

"If you do this—if you tell Coach," Brian said finally, "you'll have enemies."

Bobby thought about that for a moment, but remained silent.

"*This* is why I steer clear of these parties, man," Brian said. "Drama."

They drove the rest of the way to Brian's house in silence. Bobby dropped Brian off and on the way home, he thought about Larissa.

16

I T WAS LATE WHEN BOBBY PARKED HIS CAR INSIDE the gate in front of his house. He hustled from the car to the front door, feeling relieved once he entered the toasty confines of his home. The light was on in the kitchen. Bobby walked in and saw his dad at the kitchen table, with no drink in front of him.

"Hey, son," Mel said.

"Dad, what are you doing up this late?"

"With such a big game tomorrow, I could ask you the same thing."

Bobby didn't respond.

"Ah, I couldn't sleep," Mel said. "So I came down here to wait for you to get in."

"I got dragged to this party," Bobby said.

"Where's your sweatshirt? It's cold out tonight."

Bobby sighed. "It's a long story."

"Do you want to sit with me for a little bit?"

"Sure."

Bobby took a seat in a chair across from his father and the action felt foreign because the two of them didn't spend much time together, although the process of reversing that trend had begun recently. To Mel's credit, from the moment Bobby got the starting job, there was no extra pressure lumped onto his son's shoulders from anyone in the Dupree household, most importantly, not from Mel himself. He took secret joy in Bobby's success on the field. But there was a wide distance between Mel's personal enjoyment and expression of that joy. Mel did not know a lot about his son, just as the same was true for Bobby. Mel learned more about his son, and to a greater extent they experienced each other, by Bobby being on the field.

"You look troubled," Mel said.

Bobby opened his mouth and almost spilled the night's events outright. He thought for a moment before speaking.

"Have you ever had to do something that went against what most other people thought?" he asked. "I mean, have you ever made a decision that was unpopular among a group of people?"

"Sure, son," Mel said. "That happens in business all the time."

"Is it a hard thing to do?"

"It can be," Mel said, "depending on the nature of the decision."

"You mean, whether or not the decision is important to you?"

"Yes. If the decision is sound, the only thing that matters is how *you* feel about it. If it's important to you, and it feels right, then you make it."

Bobby watched his father and then the clock on the microwave. Mel eyed his son.

"Do you have to make an unpopular decision?" Mel asked.

"I think so."

"Are you going to?"

"Yes."

Bobby stood up from the kitchen table. He had gotten more out of this five-minute exchange with his father, than out of the last seventeen years.

"Good night, Dad," Bobby said.

"Good night, son."

. . . .

Bobby woke up the next morning with bigger things on his mind than the Katy game. He was about to drop a bomb on the entire hopes of Trinity's season, just hours before the biggest game of the season. He arrived at school an hour early. He walked into the locker room, dropped off his bag, and lingered in front of his locker before going in to talk to Stud.

He needed to gather the final dose of courage necessary for what he was about to do.

He walked to Stud's office and knocked on the half-opened door. When no response came, Bobby pushed the door open and stepped in.

Stud was sitting at his desk with the ubiquitous bulge in his lower lip.

"Bobby," he said. "You're early."

Bobby walked in with caution. Stud picked up on it and narrowed his eyes.

"I have to tell you something," Bobby said as he sat down in front of Stud.

"Sure. What is it?"

"Something happened last night, with Troy."

"Degarmo? What is it now?"

"We were at a party. Most of the guys were there. Troy was drunk and . . . "

Stud leaned in and with this action, the pressure mounted. Bobby remembered his father's advice from the night before in the kitchen and then thought about Larissa. These thoughts eased his mind. Bobby used his memory to help him with the pressure of a game—memorizing the plays during a two-minute drill or recalling the "hot" receiver on certain blitz—and he did the same with *this* pressure.

"There was a girl at the party," Bobby said. "Troy wanted to have sex with her, I guess, but she didn't want to. Troy got mad and we had to calm him down."

Stud leaned back in his chair and drew in a deep breath. "I didn't hear anything from the cops," he said. "If there was a rape involving one of my players, I would've heard about it."

"It wasn't a rape exactly," Bobby said. "She was upset. She was afraid."

"So, what do you want me to do? Why are you telling me this?" Stud asked. "My starting left tackle didn't rape a girl. He just upset her. Is that all?"

"I want you to throw Troy off the team."

Stud laughed at first but when he realized that Bobby was not kidding, his face hardened.

"We can deal with this in-house, Bobby. I'll have a talk with Troy and straighten him out. Make sure nothing like this happens again. But you can't expect me to get rid of one of the best offensive tackles in the whole state of Texas on the day of the biggest game of the season for something like this. As far as I can tell, nothing really happened. If the cops come in, and they tell me different, then—"

Bobby was unmoved by his coach's solution.

Stud shifted uncomfortably in his chair. "I mean, you said it yourself that he didn't rape her. I can't do what you're saying to do for something like this. Without proof. It sounds like a vendetta—something you and Troy need to work out."

"What?" Bobby asked. "What Troy did was wrong. The girl, her shirt was ripped. She was crying, and—"

"And you or I can't say for sure what happened," Stud said. "We weren't in the room with them."

"No Coach. He was wrong. Troy *is* wrong."

"Let me handle it, Bobby. You just need to focus on the game."

Bobby sighed deeply. "If you don't kick Troy off the team," Bobby said calmly, "I'm going to tell the principal what happened last night. What I saw last night. *And* you can count me out of tonight's game. I won't play another snap with Troy as a teammate."

Stud was paralyzed by the sureness of Bobby's ultimatum. The timing stunned him as well. And without time to react, Stud couldn't get angry *and* deal with the situation. There was simply no room for both.

Bobby stood up from the chair in front of Stud's desk.

"You let me know what you decide, Coach," Bobby said. "I'll be in the locker room."

. . . .

Stud made the only decision that was available to him. He met with the young girl and heard her story. Then, about two hours before kickoff, Stud called Degarmo into his office and explained to him that he was suspended from school—meaning he could not play football—and that the decision was effective immediately. He did not specify that it was Bobby who had told him about what happened at the party, but Degarmo knew that already. Stud also told his star left tackle that the reason for his dismissal would not be made public until the following week because an investigation would have to take place first. To the public, Troy would miss the Katy game due to injury.

Troy was devastated and his first impulse was to enter the locker room and take revenge on Bobby. But before he was able to do so, the school's director of security cut him off at the pass and explained that if he came after Bobby, he would find himself permanently off the team and facing charges.

. . . .

With thirty minutes left before kickoff, the entire

locker room was aware of the decision regarding Degarmo. The players on the team who knew Degarmo, who had enjoyed the party the night before, and had gone through battles with him on the field, were angry at Stud's decision, and specifically, angry at Bobby. This faction of the team couldn't comprehend how Bobby could sell out one of his teammates.

But there were two very important teammates in Bobby's corner: Brian Bell and Tyrone Gilliam.

Bobby sat in front of his locker, glaring back in defiance at all the hard stares he received. Brian came by before hitting the field. He pounded fists with Bobby.

"Don't sweat it," he said. "You did the right thing. Let's go get this win."

Bobby nodded and wiped the sweat off his forehead.

Tyrone Gilliam followed shortly behind Brian.

"I heard about last night with Troy," Tyrone said. "I got your back, Dupree."

Bobby smiled.

"For the righteous falls seven times and rises again, but the wicked stumble in times of calamity," Tyrone added.

They shook hands and Tyrone left the locker room. Bobby closed his eyes and took a deep breath. He grabbed his helmet and took the field.

17

TRINITY TOOK THE FIELD AS A TEAM DIVIDED, WITH Bobby Dupree in the eye of the storm. The disgruntled members of the team who were on Degarmo's side would never dare view Brian and Tyrone as deserters—mainly because of their pedigrees on the field and statures within the locker room. Their anger was directed at one person and one person only.

The stands inside Pennington Field were packed. There wasn't an empty space to be had, standing room or otherwise. The cowboy hats were visible, set up in a front row camp right behind Trinity's sideline. As news of Degarmo's absence spread, the rumors ranged from Troy punching out a teammate in the locker room to him being diagnosed with cancer. Such was the curious nature of embellishment within the crowd.

As Bobby waited on the sideline for the opening kickoff, the cheering section for each side began its respective school's chant. The result was a wall of sound that surrounded and enveloped the green space between. Bobby tried to block it all out. He closed his eyes and thought that Larissa would be proud of him. If only she knew.

Trinity was to receive the ball first and their sideline erupted in jubilation when Katy's kicker sent the opening kickoff out of bounds. Without playing a snap, Trinity was in business. First and ten from its own forty-yard line.

Before Bobby trotted out onto the field, Stud pulled him aside.

"Throw it away if it's not there," Stud said. "Stay focused."

Bobby nodded and stepped onto the field. He made his way over to the huddle, and the only set of eyes on him belonged to Brian. Trinity broke the huddle and Bobby looked out at the Katy defense before getting under center. He called out his cadence, put Brian in motion, and took the snap. As soon as he dropped back to pass, a walloping hit came from the blind side—the spot that Degarmo had manned for the first four games. Not only did the sack push Trinity back ten yards, but it also knocked the wind out of Bobby. After just one play, he had to be peeled off the turf by Brian. None of the offensive lineman had even given it a thought to help Bobby up.

In the huddle before second down, Bobby struggled to take hold of his breathing and call out the play. At that moment he realized that it would be a miracle to play well in this game because he would have to defeat two teams.

On second down, Bobby handed the ball off to Tevin on a delay and he gained fourteen yards up the left side. Third and six. Bobby called the next play in the huddle—a deep shot to Brian. He knew to be alert for quick pressure this time. At the line of scrimmage, Bobby eyed the right defensive end, the player going up against Degarmo's replacement. He saw that the defender was raring to get off on the snap. Bobby gave a hard count and the right defensive end jumped offside. Because the end did not make contact with an offensive player, Trinity had a free play. Bobby realized this and took the snap. He dropped back and launched the ball in Brian's direction, as far as he could. Brian separated from the corner, and at the last moment, ran underneath the pass. Touchdown Trinity, on a heads-up play from Bobby.

Bobby ran down the field like a madman. He was so excited that he tackled Brian in the end zone. The ref warned him for excessive celebration, but he didn't care. The play was a validation; he had earned the right to express a little joy.

The score marked Bobby's eleventh touchdown

pass of the season, and Brian's ninth TD catch. Aside from their obvious connection on the field, their bond off it was solid too.

Before Trinity kicked it off to Katy, its sideline was awash in euphoria. The crowd called out to Bobby, professing its undying love for him. One female fan went so far as to ask him for his hand in marriage. If only the crowd knew that Bobby was at odds with the majority of the people he was leading.

Bobby walked over to Stud and pulled his helmet off.

"You know the sack happened on purpose, right?" Bobby asked. "The first play of the game."

Stud looked out onto the field, spat a chunky, brown glob onto the grass, and *then* looked at his quarterback. "I didn't see it that way," he said. "I just saw our *backup* offensive tackle, who, by the way, had no first team reps this week, get beat by an all-state defensive end. Just play the game. You made a hell of a play. Build on it."

Bobby nodded and slipped his helmet back on.

Stud turned his attention back onto the field and Bobby found a spot on the sideline, as far away as possible from Stud and the rest of his team.

Katy scored to even it up at seven with a ten-play, eighty-yard drive that ate up the rest of the first quarter.

Bobby took the field after the kickoff and walked into the huddle. There was still no eye contact from anyone inside the huddle other than Brian.

"Listen up, I want you guys to know that if you let your man beat you on purpose, and I get planted into the ground . . . "

He had the huddle's attention now.

"That I'm gonna get up. Every time. And I'm either gonna win this game with you or without you. I know you don't like what happened with Troy. But forget about him. *We* are here together and we can win this game together. We don't need Troy."

His teammates only stared in response without

saying a word. Bobby didn't know if he had reached them, but at least he had eye contact.

The offense approached the line of scrimmage. Bobby tried to draw Katy offside with another hard count, but one of the offensive lineman jumped instead, costing Trinity five yards.

After the penalty, Bobby received the next play for a freshman wide receiver who was rotating in. He called the play on one, so there wouldn't be any confusion amongst the offensive line. Trinity broke the huddle sloppily; wandering to the line of scrimmage one by one, instead of as one.

"Blue thirty-eight! Blue thirty-eight! Go!"

Bobby took the snap and looked to the left, where both receivers were covered. The pocket collapsed around him, and he slipped out to the left by giving ground to the oncoming rush. The receiver in the left flat broke off his route and headed up the field. Bobby stopped, planted his feet, and launched the pass down the left sideline. The intended receiver almost tripped over his own feet as the ball came his way. He caught it, barely, with the ball nearly slipping through his hands. Instead of walking in for a touchdown, a pursuing Katy defender tripped him up at the five. Bobby didn't see the result of the play because, as he released the ball, a defensive lineman put all of his six-foot-two height and one hundred ninety-five pounds into him.

He could tell from the crowd's reaction that something had gone right for Trinity. No one helped him up off the turf. He picked himself up and joined the rest of the offense on the doorstep of Katy's end zone. Stud sent the next play in via hand signal. It was an off-tackle run to Tevin. In the huddle, not one lineman thanked Bobby for sticking his body on the line nor asked if he was alright from the crushing hit. Brian tapped him on the back of the helmet. He knew his quarterback was tough, but was uneasy about where this could lead.

After favoring his right shoulder at the line of scrimmage, Bobby snapped the ball and handed it off to Tevin. The back stopped in his tracks, as Katy stuffed the gap. He bounced the run to the outside, and from there it was a race to the front pylon. From a yard out, Tevin dove head first and broke the plane of the goal line. The side judge raised two arms into the air. Touchdown. Trinity was up fourteen to seven after the extra point.

As soon as Bobby reached the sideline, Trinity's trainer got a hold of him and began examining his right shoulder.

"What happened on the play?" the trainer asked.

"He lifted me and fell right on top of my shoulder," Bobby said, wincing through the prods from the trainer's fingers.

"There's no range of motion," the trainer said.

Bobby tried to lift his right shoulder over his head, but couldn't. It burned with any movement. He then felt a crunching sensation, as he lowered the arm to his side.

"It's strained badly. If not torn," the trainer said. "You gotta come out."

"Hold on," Bobby said, grabbing the trainer's

arm with his off arm. He did not want out of the game. Not *this* game. Not with all that was going on. He wanted to be a part of this. He wanted to be a part of something bigger than himself. He had been on the bench before and knew what that was like. But now that he had a little taste of something else and didn't want it to end. Bobby didn't want to go back to riding the bench.

"I'm fine," Bobby pleaded. "Just give it the chance to loosen up. I'll be fine. It's just pain."

The trainer looked into Bobby's eyes and knew full well the risk in allowing the injured quarterback to continue playing. The look in Bobby's eyes meant much more than his words. The look was an appeal.

"Okay," the trainer said. "You be straight with me, though. If it gets to the point where you can't protect yourself out there, you have to tell me!"

The trainer eyed Bobby sternly.

"I mean it," he said.

"I promise," Bobby said.

During the time that Bobby was with the trainer,

Katy had driven down to Trinity's twenty-yard line. Bobby walked to a vantage point on the sideline where he could get a good look at the next snap. He resisted the urge to rub his right shoulder as he watched.

Katy's quarterback snapped the ball and faked a handoff to his tailback. When Trinity's aggressive linebackers bit on the fake, there was a wide open lane to throw the drag route across the middle to the tight end. Katy's QB released the pass and hit his tight end in stride. The tight end ran into the end zone. After the extra point, the score was knotted up at fourteen.

There were thirty-five seconds left in the first half. Though the trainer kept his word to Bobby, Stud knew that Bobby's throwing shoulder had to be sore. He saw the shots that Bobby took during the first two quarters and also noticed out of the corner of his eye, how Bobby was favoring his shoulder on the side line. Though Bobby hid it well, Stud was an ex-quarterback himself. He knew how a quarterback stood when trying to mask an injury, and was also familiar with the pain of being pulled from a game due to that injury.

Stud thought hard as Trinity waited for the ensuing kickoff. He sized Bobby up outright now. He thought about pulling Bobby out of the game at halftime. His dilemma was a difficult one. One that could shape his future. Stud wasn't debating pulling Bobby simply because of the shoulder injury. Bobby's injury provided an opportunity. With the stunt that Bobby pulled before the game, how could Stud trust him now? If Bobby would have just given him until after the game to deal with Degarmo, the situation would have been manageable. As it was, the kid had put Stud in an impossible spot and he was pissed off about it. Still, Bobby was Stud's best quarterback on the roster. Mickey Montoya wasn't ready to play. Especially not in the Katy game.

Stud needed Bobby. He was on shaky ground with Trinity's boosters, the ones in the cowboy hats with the itchy trigger fingers. Stud had to win and he had to win now. But Bobby had ruined it. He went against one of his own, thereby putting his entire team in jeopardy. How could Stud trust Bobby? He couldn't. Stud made his decision as he watched his renegade signal caller; he whistled shrilly in Pete's direction. Pete caught the sound and paced over to Stud.

"What's up?" Pete asked, wired from the competition on the field, buzzed from the extra-large dip he fitted onto his bottom lip during the first half.

Stud leaned in close. "I'm taking Bobby out at half time."

"What?"

"His shoulder."

"The trainer said he was fine."

"He's not fine," Stud said, flashing to the moment before the game, when Bobby sandbagged him in his office. "It doesn't matter anyway, Pete. Dupree is not a winner. You think we could win a state title with Dupree at quarterback? We wouldn't win one playoff game."

Pete didn't respond because Stud's words reeked of stinky, self-serving rationalization. They stunk of fear and revenge. Pete had nothing to add to the unilateral decision that Stud had made, and instead elected to pace down the sideline, away from the stench.

"Bobby!" Stud called out, after Trinity ran the kickoff out to the forty-five yard line, injecting life back into its home crowd. "Sit on it! Let's get in the locker room!"

"Sit on it?" Bobby said, waving a hand out to the field. "Look at the field position! We have two timeouts!"

"We're gonna play it this way, Dupree!"

"My shoulder's fine!" Bobby wailed.

"Sit on the goddamn ball!"

Bobby buttoned his chinstrap and ran out onto the field with his head hanging low. Stud had made his decision. Bobby just didn't know it yet.

He snapped the ball and knelt down to salt away the remaining seconds of the first half. Trinity's crowd, which a moment earlier was jubilant, now rained boos down onto Stud—boos he avoided by sprinting into the locker room ahead of his players. Bobby walked off the field and when he neared the stands, the crowd chanted his name.

. . . .

Bobby spent the first ten minutes of the twelve-minute half with the trainer.

"Did you tell Stud about my arm?" Bobby asked.

"I told Pete you dinged it," the trainer said, avoiding Bobby's eyes. "They had to know already anyway."

Bobby eyed the trainer with caution.

"I'm thinking about giving you a shot," the trainer said. "How's the pain?"

"It's still there," Bobby said. "It only burns when there's direct contact to it."

"That's good. You'll be safe from direct contact on a football field," the trainer joked.

Bobby had heard how shots can lead to bigger problems for players. There was one prominent Trinity player from the recent past who took a pain-killing shot to the knee before every game during his junior season and by the time his senior campaign rolled around, the former Trinity star was hooked on prescription painkillers.

"I don't want it," Bobby said. "I'll just . . . "

The trainer looked at him without blinking. A sheet of sweat formed on his forehead.

"Deal with it," Bobby said.

"Remember what I told you earlier," the trainer said, rubbing Icy Hot on the damaged shoulder. "You have to be honest with me. That's how this works. I'm honest with you, you're honest with me."

"Yeah." Bobby yipped with pain as the trainer hit a nerve.

"I'm finishing this game," Bobby said, standing up from a massage table that stood in for an examination table and taping station. He looked for his shoulder pads and found them on the floor.

He placed the armor onto his shoulders. The right shoulder burned with persistence and Bobby did his best to mask the pain by not letting it show on his face. The gesture was moot; the trainer already knew that the shoulder injury was more than a "ding," a legitimate problem in fact. He just hoped Bobby would make it out of the game in one piece. Bobby's view of the situation was one of relishing the warrior mentality; you couldn't say you were a football player until you risked your health to get onto the field. Bobby could check that box off now.

He caught a glimpse of himself in the full-body mirror in the trainer's room. His uniform was filthy; dirt and grass stains everywhere, a smear of blood across his thigh pad from a cut on his left hand. Bobby remembered so many games where after the clock hit zero, his uniform was clean. He looked up into the mirror and his face was unrecognizable. His eyes were razors, alert and discerning. His hair was matted with sweat and the black under his eyes had run down his cheeks. Bobby smiled like a wild man, a young warrior who was just coming into his own, just coming of age. He looked back to the trainer who figured Bobby for arrogant, dumb or just old-fashioned crazy. Or maybe some combination of all three.

"This is how it's supposed to be," Bobby said. "This is how it feels to be a part of it."

Bobby walked out of the trainer's room and tried to make it straight onto the field, but Stud stopped him at the door.

"I need to talk to you, Bobby," Stud said, with tired eyes.

Bobby didn't understand how Stud's eyes could be so lifeless at a time like this.

"*Talk?*" Bobby said.

. . . .

By this point, most of the players were back on the field, readying for the second half. A few lingered in the locker room though, eyes widened with intrigue.

Stud looked around the locker room.

"The rest of you get your asses onto the field!"

The contingent of malingerers darted out. All except Brian Bell. He waited, tying up his cleats slowly. Stud would never raise his voice to Brian directly.

"What's up, Coach?" Bobby asked quietly.

Stud gathered himself with a couple of deep breaths.

"Bobby," Stud said. "I'm gonna go with Mickey in the second half."

A wave of rage ran through Bobby's heart, and his eyes locked onto Stud's to figure out if his coach was kidding or not. Stud's expression was blank. There was no emotion in it.

"I'm telling you!" Bobby exploded. "My shoulder is fine!"

Bobby moved it around and swallowed the pain that came with the display. Stud was unmoved.

"My shoulder," Bobby said, a nausea fermenting in his gut from the pain. "My shoulder is . . . it's on fire."

And then there was the silence that marked

Bobby and Stud's relationship from the moment Edmond went down. Stud didn't trust Bobby from the beginning. And he certainly couldn't trust him now. Whereas the distrust at the beginning of the season was based on the simple fact that Bobby had never done anything other than hold a clipboard for any team he had ever played, this new iteration was forged the moment when Bobby walked into Stud's office that morning of the Katy game. Bobby had illustrated to Stud that he could not be a part of the team.

"This isn't even about my shoulder," Bobby said. "You can't get the rest of the guys to forget about Troy, can you? You can't forget either."

Stud was silent.

"Or won't?" Bobby added.

"Can't," Stud said. "There's a difference."

And Bobby understood. Now he understood.

Just as quickly as the anger came, it melted away and Bobby's posture, face and tone went back to default.

"I understand," Bobby said.

"Good," Stud said.

"Is that it?"

"That's it," Stud said. "I hope you'll consider helping Mickey the rest of the way. This game and the rest of the season. If you want to leave the team, I understand. It's up to you."

Bobby stayed silent.

"You did a hell of a job out there, Bobby," Stud said. "I want you to know that. I want you to hear it from me. You're a good player."

The sound of the crowd indicated that the second half had started. Stud shook his head at what chaos awaited him out there.

Stud walked right by Brian Bell, who had been watching the entire exchange. Brian didn't move when Stud passed him on his way to the field. Brian walked over to Bobby instead.

"I'm actually kind of glad Stud did that," Brian said. "It was getting to be a dangerous situation out there for you."

"Nah," Bobby said. "I could've handled it. I did handle it."

The boos from Trinity's crowd had reached the locker room.

18

THE NEXT MORNING, THE SUN ROSE IN DALLAS, and all of the local papers wrote it the same way: a vastly superior Katy team squeaked out a win over a Trinity squad that was more than game, led by a valiant backup quarterback named Bobby Dupree, who if not for an injured shoulder, had certainly conjured enough magic to pull the upset and cement it as one of largest and most improbable in Texas High School history.

Stud's official word to the press would be that Bobby's demotion to backup was brought on by a damaged shoulder that would endanger him out on the field and put his health in harm's way. Stud was sure to emphasize the word "serious" for effect. Stud also added that there would no doubt be growing pains with Mickey Montoya at quarterback. Off the record, Stud knew that the offense would be ground to a screeching halt in the majority of Trinity's remaining games. But in Stud's mind *this* was the only way. The other way—Bobby's way—was not sustainable. True, the season would be a failure without a trip to the playoffs. That was the minimum standard at Trinity. But the boosters wouldn't hang Stud out to dry after a season in which his star quarterback went down with a torn ACL and his upstart backup, who played beyond competency, went out with an injured rotator cuff. The what-if game would save Stud. Self-preservation came naturally to him. He had the script all written out in his mind before he even spoke to Bobby at halftime.

Bobby walked onto the field where, just a few days before, he had experienced his version of athletic nirvana, and then rock bottom, respectively, all in the span of thirty minutes. It was a rush being out there on the field, leading his team and playing well. Throw in the fact that his teammates were staging a mutiny against him, and it was no wonder that Bobby was wired for the balance of the weekend. And after a brief fling with depression on Sunday, the sun was out and shining on Monday morning. And it was silvery and bright and hot, like it always was at that time of year in Dallas. And you didn't want to look into the sun for too long thereby risking your eye sight. Bobby remembered his mother always saying that to him, while he was on the sideline in "pee-wee" and Pop Warner. Never in the game. Always with extra time to spare. Time enough to look up into the sky and damage his eye sight forever.

He went up into the stands, on Trinity's side, and sat in a seat in the front row, fifty-yard line. He looked out at Pennington Field and adjusted his shoulder, so that it rested at an angle that would not cause discomfort. Bobby wanted this moment. He was sad that the ride was over, but still wanted to remember the good parts of it. The command of the huddle, when the eyes looking back at him actually wanted to be led. The smell of the grass on a Friday night under the lights, after it's been watered and pampered all week in advance of the show. And finally, throwing to Brian Bell. Of all the things he'd miss, he'd miss throwing touchdown passes to Brian Bell. One day in the future, when Brian Bell was playing on Saturdays and then maybe even Sundays, Bobby would be sure to remember that he'd played a tiny role in helping him get there.

Bobby stood up from his front row seat; he shifted the wrong way and the bum shoulder stung him, like a blitzing linebacker from the backside. He rubbed his shoulder gently in an effort to put out the fire. But it was no use. The shoulder was messed up. It needed a rest. And it would get one.

He thought about Larissa briefly then as he looked over Pennington Field one last time. The thought of her quickly dissipated and his mind shifted back to football. Bobby punched the air with his left hand, cursing the fact that he didn't see that nickel-back in the flat, during one practice early in the season. The meaningless interception would always eat at him.

. . . .

In school that day, Bobby was taking the demotion just fine. He had spent the weekend resting with his family. They took the news in stride while taking tremendous pride in his play. Bobby played up the shoulder angle rather than tell the truth to his family. True, it was the easy way out. But the people involved that *needed* to know the truth, did in fact, know it. Bobby was called into the principal's office at Trinity early Monday morning to give his statement regarding the incident with Degarmo. He gave the investigators the whole truth, withholding nothing, beholden to nothing other than what was right.

Trinity High School's varsity football team was Mickey Montoya's problem now. Bobby would offer his assistance to Mickey when possible—if and when the shoulder allowed it—but Bobby knew better than anyone now that once the job is yours, it's yours and yours alone.

After his third period Civics class, Bobby crossed paths with Larissa in front his locker. His shoulder was in a sling now. Truthfully, it had improved enough over the weekend to ditch the sling, but Stud wanted to lay it on thick, and Bobby agreed that that was probably best. When Larissa stopped in front of his locker, Bobby slammed it shut with his back. They made eye contact and both chuckled, their nervous energies getting the best of them.

"Hey," Larissa said.

"Hey," Bobby said.

"How's the shoulder?"

"It's fine," he said. "It's weird doing some things though."

She laughed again as he shrugged the tied-down appendage.

The crowd in the hall thinned out, and soon Larissa and Bobby had the entire space to themselves.

"I heard what you did at that party," Larissa said.

Bobby didn't say anything and set his eyes to the floor.

"It was really courageous of you," she said.

Bobby looked up at Larissa and stared into her eyes for the first time. He felt that finally, he was able to do so without feeling strange or insecure. He had earned it.

"To tell you the truth," Bobby said. "It didn't feel courageous when I did it. Even that night of the party, when everyone there was looking at me and my teammates were pissed at me. I just did it."

Larissa smiled. "Still," she said, "I wanted you to know that."

The bell rung and their free time was coming to an end.

"Well," she said, "gotta go."

"Hey Larissa," Bobby said. "Can I take you out some time? To a movie or to grab a burger or something?"

"I don't think so," she said. "I don't go out with football players, remember?"

Bobby lifted his right shoulder. "Well you should know," he said. "I'm technically not a football player anymore. I'm back to riding the bench."

Larissa laughed, but sweetly. "How about I say, *maybe*," she said.

Bobby opened his mouth to reply, but the words had escaped him.

"Bye Bobby," she said.

"Bye Larissa."

Larissa Mumphrey left Bobby alone in front of his locker and now he was late for class. But it was okay. The old shoulder in the sling getup would buy him a few extra minutes with his teachers at Trinity.

He made his way down the hall at a steady pace, looking at the football team's trophies and memorabilia, housed in cases that lined both sides of the hallway. Bobby didn't feel sad about the fact that there would be no public memory of his contribution to Trinity's rich football history. He knew what he had added.